# Not Another Day
## stories and poetry

### by

# Julius Chingono

Published by Weaver Press, Box A1922, Avondale, Harare. 2006

Typeset by Weaver Press
Cover Design: Xealos, Harare

The publishers w̲ ̲ ̲ ̲ gratitude to Hivos for the support they have
given to Weaver Press in the development of their fiction
programme.

This collection of stories is a work of fiction and a product of the author's imagination.
The author's use of the names of actual places is intended to change the entirely fic-
tional character of the work. Any current references of the text to persons living is purely
coincidental.

ISBN:1-77922-048-0
ISBN-13: 978-1-77922-048-6

**Julius Chingono** was born on a commercial farm in 1946,and has worked for most of his life on the mines as a blaster. He has had his poetry published in several anthologies of Shona poetry including *Nhetembo, Mabvumira eNhetembo* and *Gwenyambira* between 1968 and 1980. His only novel, *Chipo Changu* was published in 1978 and an award-winning play, *Ruvimbo*, was published in 1980. His poetry in English has also been published in several South African and Zimbabwean anthologies: *Flags of Love (Mireza yerudo)*(1983) and *Flag of Rags* (1996). He has contributed to Poetry International in the Netherlands.

# Contents

## Short Stories

1. Tomorrow is not another day     1

2. 'Are we together?'     15

3. New beginnings     25

4. Sisters-in-law     33

5. Amai Takawira     49

6. Sahwira's condoms     59

7. The funeral     69

8. An early supper     87

9. The commuter     105

10. The employment agent     113

Glossary     123

## Poetry

My Sekai     11

Colour blind     12

The Accident     13

The African sun     14

Heroes     23

The Merc     24

Ode to a tree     31

Christmas Day News     32

Untitled     44

If it's not     45

| | |
|---|---|
| I do love, I do | 46 |
| Subjects | 47 |
| Some people | 48 |
| Englished | 57 |
| All is not well | 58 |
| Occasional sex | 66 |
| The shoes of a vagabond | 67 |
| Deceased | 68 |
| I do not want to be mother | 84 |
| Commission of Inquiry | 86 |
| Shrapnel | 102 |
| Recipe | 103 |
| Victoria Falls | 104 |
| Run black girl | 110 |
| In the beginning | 111 |
| From a painting | 112 |
| She | 122 |

# 1

# Tomorrow is not another day

A *blue landcruiser* bumped slowly along the rough road that ran along the edge of a footpath that led to an isolated homestead tucked beneath a range of hills. The heavy vehicle bounced across a makeshift bridge of stones and logs that straddled a small stream which sprang from the hills and flowed down into a vlei of stunted winter grass and patches of scrub.

As they approached, a small boy emerged from the smallest hut and stood quietly watching the adults climb out of the landcruiser. He gave no sign of recognition.

'Masimba! Masimba!' called a large dark woman in a yellow dress stretching her arms expansively and rushing towards the child. The boy did not move. 'Are you forgetting me, Masimba?' She enveloped the small figure with her big frame. The boy shrank in her embrace. He held a ball made of rags, paper and plastic in one hand while the other held up his oversize trousers that would certainly have dropped down had he not done so. 'Masimba. Look at me.' The woman gripped his shoulders, squeezing him slightly. She looked into his face. 'Do you recognise me now?'

Slowly, but sadly, the boy nodded his head and looked away.

Her companions, two men and one woman, walked over to join her. The driver of the landcruiser remained in his vehicle making notes. The adults observed the boy as he hesitated before responding to the large woman who continued to smile and squeeze his shoulder in a friendly manner. His shirt had no buttons, it was torn at the shoulders and was very dirty. It was also evident that he had not taken a bath for a long time.

'Masimba, I've brought you some food and clothes.' The woman was desperate for a favourable response. Masimba stretched out an open palm and his trousers dropped to his feet. He did not seem to mind.

'Cathy, get me a box of chips and chicken please.'

'Whose box? OK, I'll donate my lunch,' Cathy said taking a few hesitant steps towards the 4x4.

'This is not the time to think ...' The big woman bent down as if to draw up the boy's trousers and cover his small bony thighs.

'You did not take us with you,' Masimba said suddenly, his voice hardly audible, looking the woman in the face for the first time.

'I wanted to get some things for you ... but where is your sister?' Masimba opened his mouth but did not say anything. 'He has an older sister, Fungai.' She addressed the group behind her. A bespectacled man in corduroy trousers held up with braces took a notebook from his shirt pocket.

'How old is Masimba?' He sounded as if he was not part of the group. He chewed his lower lip as he listened.

'Seven years old.' The man scribbled in his notebook.

Cathy returned with some food wrapped in a plastic bag. She gave it to the boy who, putting down his ball, received the package tentatively and began to unwrap it.

'The sister?' The man bent forward towards Masimba as if he intended to interview him. 'Can we find somewhere to sit?'

'The sister is Fungai ... she is nine.' The big woman looked at the man expecting further questions.

'Both of them ... are they going to school?'

'No. Cathy, bring some water. He cannot eat with such dirty hands. This is a terrible situation which ...' The woman's voice faded away as the spectacled man interrupted.

'When did you last come here?' His voice exuded authority. He sounded accusatory. It seemed as if he already knew the answer but wanted her to give it.

'Last month but one, about six, seven weeks ago.' They regarded each other accusingly until she looked away. 'I had no transport, Edward ... you know the situation at head office.' Her voice was loud but uncertain. The man fussed with his pen as he wrote in his notebook.

Then, taking the boy by the hand, he led him to the vehicle. 'Theresa, come along.' It was a command. Theresa, the woman in the yellow dress, followed, shaking her head as if she was dealing with a hopeless situation. It looked as if the man had wrested the leadership role from her.

Cathy meantime wandered over to join the other member of their group, a young man who was surveying the compound. The kitchen-hut faced the one that was used as the bedroom. It was dusty and potholed. There were no kitchen utensils. A shelf moulded onto the wall and a hearth at the centre was enough evidence as to the purpose of the hut. The fireplace was empty. There was no door. Cathy, who was a thin woman with a sad face, also recorded her observations in her small book. There was no shortage of notebooks.

'How have these children survived ... there's no food?' Cathy asked.

'There are no doors! 'The young man beside her said unnecessarily as though he enjoyed stating the obvious.

'And just one torn blanket!' He sounded as if he had made some great historical discovery though his tone was not triumphant.

'Theresa says the children live here alone,' Cathy continued, peering into the hut, which seemed only to house a large colony of ants.

'Her report states that they sold their few belongings to raise money for food. Their parents died three years ago.'

'This is a worse situation than the one we dealt with in Shamva,' the young man commented, stooping to get a better view of the hut. 'How come this case was not attended to sooner?' he asked.

'There was no fuel. Gary, you know how it is.'

'There are fuel reserves for such cases, you know that.' The man pierced the air between them with his forefinger emphasising his point.

'Beside the fuel problem …,' Cathy looked around and lowered her voice. 'This constituency was won by the opposition in the last elections.' She stopped again, looking around fearfully, as if she expected men with dark glasses to pounce on her. 'The government is not distributing food here.' Her last words were scarcely audible, as she turned to make her way quickly back to the landcruiser.

Edward and Theresa had found themselves a patch of grass on which to sit near the 4x4. They spread a canvas sheet and newspapers on top of the grass. Masimba ate with speed and relish. Theresa dared not disturb him with questions.

'I still cannot figure out how these children are still alive. They have no food, no blankets and no clothes,' the younger man, Gary, said joining his colleagues on the grass.

'Gary, did you not read my report? … I thought I'd highlighted the situation as one requiring immediate attention,' Theresa replied. Gary, who was making himself a seat with a piece of newspaper, did not deign to reply. Theresa paged through a file of papers. 'The problem with you social workers is that you are no longer shocked when you read the reports. You have lost all feeling.' She handed the file to her young colleague who looked the other way.

Masimba began to cough.

'Give that child some drinking water, he is choking.' Gary wiped his eyes. Cathy, who was leaning against the vehicle stretched inside and grabbed a plastic cup. She threw it to Theresa who failed to catch it. Everyone laughed except the young man who looked as if he was praying.

'Well … there is work to be done here,' Edward said, assuming his leadership role.

Masimba drank his water and continued to eat with undiminished appetite.

'There is not much we can do here. Are you aware that this is an opposition party constituency?' Theresa asked. The younger man raised an opened palm which had its intended effect, Theresa fell silent. Then getting up, he walked slowly away, his hands in his jeans' pockets.

'This job can be very stressful', Edward commented, loudly enough for Gary to hear. 'It is not a job for over-sensitive people.'

'The sister … er … er … where can she be?' He continued, changing the subject, having made his point.

'Do let the child finish eating, Edward,' Theresa cautioned irritably.

'What time is it?... Maybe she is out looking for food. ' Cathy suggested, opening the door of the landcruiser and moving to sit on the front seat.

'Masimba, where is your sister? What's her name?'

'Fungai ... Edward let him finish. He's almost through,' said Theresa.

The older man looked very obviously at his watch, but said nothing.

In the silence that followed they all watched Gary, who could be seen moving in and out of the two empty huts as if he was searching for something.

'She went with vaHove who gave us food,' Masimba's small voice broke the silence.

'Where's that?' Edward rose as if he wanted to lead the group there immediately.

'Do you know where vaHove lives?'

'Yes, behind that hill.' He spoke with a mouth full of chicken.

'When did they leave?' Cathy joined in the interrogation from her position in the vehicle.

'Last month,' the child responded pointing northwards with a drum stick.

'Do you sleep alone then?' Cathy continued, her face drawn, 'I don't like this at all.'

'No. I sleep with Never, our neighbour across the stream. I only come back here in the morning.' Masimba answered, the food seeming to have given him a little courage.

'Can we reach there in the cruiser?' Edward moved towards the 4x4. Nobody replied. 'Masimba, can we drive to vaHove's home in the car?' Edward's voice was loud and impatient. Masimba recoiled.

'There's no need to shout, Edward,' Theresa said, coming to Masimba's rescue. Then she turned to the child, 'Is it near ... can we walk to vaHove's home?'

'Very near.' Masimba rose unsteadily.

'Wash your hands first.' Theresa poured some water over his outstretched palms and the boy washed hurriedly and then grabbed at his trousers.

'Can't someone find something to hold up those trousers? Gary said irritably as he rejoined the group.

'You do something, Gary.' Edward replied, and Gary fumbled in his pockets uselessly.

'Let's find Masimba's sister … which way Masimba?'

The child ran ahead and the adults followed down the path behind him. Edward rolled up the sleeves of his shirt as though he was advancing into battle. Gary trailed behind sniffing as though he was near to tears.

They followed a footpath that meandered round big grey boulders; musasa and mupfuti trees flanked the edge of the hillside. The grass was short and stunted. It was a forest with no inhibitions. After a while, a small, scarcely used, path branched to their right and Masimba followed it.

After about fifteen minutes they arrived at a homestead consisting of four pole and dagga huts. The thatch was refurbished and new. The brown walls of the huts were hand polished. The yard had no weeds. An orchard of mango, peach, avocado pear and guava trees was conspicuous with its huge aged trees. A wet garden of green vegetables and unripe tomatoes lay visible behind the huts. They approached a hut with an open door. Masimba obviously knew the homestead well.

Gary moved from behind and fell in beside Edward at the front. Slowing down, the party from Harare blocked the doorway. They were silent for a minute, before peering into the hut.

'Knock! For goodness sake, show some respect, Gary.' The man with spectacles moved forward and knocked forcefully on the door

'Respect child abusers …' Gary muttered.

Masimba walked into the hut and looked behind the half-open door.

'Fungai! Fungai!' He called out fearlessly as if he was in his own bedroom. Gary followed the boy into the hut.

The child had crouched down beside what appeared to be a body of a child covered with a blanket. Edward stood erect beside him.

The women stood silently outside.

'Fungai! Wake up!' Masimba casually pulled the worn out grey blanket away from the small body that lay beneath it.

'My God! What's this?' Edward drew back two steps. Gary stooped forward.

'She's dead … she … Theresa!' Edward shouted again pulling Masimba away. Gary covered his face with his hands.

A face stared up at them. The eyes were so wide open they seemed to have rolled out of their sockets. Blood seeped from the nostrils which were still wet; a gaping mouth exposed small white teeth. A smell of faeces wafted from the blanket. Edward knelt beside the body. He felt the pulse.

Theresa walked into the hut, opening her mouth to speak but nobody heard what she wanted to say.

'Is this Fungai?' Edward asked Theresa who had retreated back to the door. 'She's dead but her body is still warm.' He rose.

Theresa hesitantly stepped towards the body, and kneeling forward cried, '*Mai-mai-maiwee,*' then covered her eyes with her hands. 'Is this the girl?' Edward asked insistently, leading Masimba gently out of the hut.

'I do not know. I never saw her.'

Outside the hut they looked at each other and then looked at Masimba who seemed confused.

'When did you last talk to Fungai, Masimba?' Edward asked, his voice gentle.

'Yesterday. I spoke to her yesterday, but she could not walk. She said her legs were painful,' Masimba explained. Theresa was weeping quietly. 'Is she dead?' Masimba asked, but no one answered. Edward looked at his watch and jotted something in his notebook.

Gary moved back inside the hut, covered the body with the blanket, and gently closed the child's eyes.

'What did she do to deserve such an end?' he said unsteadily, as he returned to join his colleagues. His distress was so obvious that Cathy wanted to hold and steady him. 'Who did this?' he cried again.

'I should have come back earlier,' Theresa wailed. 'I should have …'

'It is not our fault …' Cathy said firmly trying to instill some reality into a situation that looked as if it might get out of hand. 'Nonetheless, what we must ask is how and why she died?

'Masimba, did you see vaHove here yesterday?' she continued.

'No.' Masimba answered, adding, 'Fungai told me vaHove had gone to look for some medicine to cure her legs.'

Edward moved back into the hut and pulled the blanket right off the girl. She was naked. Her pelvic area was swollen and pus had seeped from her pubis, which was hairless as if it had been shaven.

'How can some man in his right mind take a child and have sex with her?' Gary burst out as if it was he who was examining Fungai's body. No one replied. He paced up and down in front of the hut as if he could barely control his emotions. Masimba observed him with amazement.

'Gary, what has got into you?' Edward asked as he came out of the hut.

'Do you not appreciate that this is first degree murder!' Gary paused in his tracks for a moment.

'That is for the courts to decide.' Edward said firmly.

'No one is here for these young ... these children ... even you social workers are good for nothing.' Gary looked Edward in the face. 'Can you imagine what that child went through before she was strangled?' His face was wet with tears and he seemed to have shrunk into his safari suit. He pushed Edward aside and again began to pace to and fro as if this was the only way of managing his surging feelings.

'How can we strategise when people can't behave?' Edward's barbed question was directed at Theresa who seemed to have recovered a little.

'Leave him alone.' Theresa sniffed several times, dropping her wet tissues on the ground.

'Strategise? What strategy? It is too late for strategy. These children need protection.' Gary paused, jerking his head as he saw a heavily built man approaching from the vegetable garden. 'Are you vaHove? He? He?'

The man walked dejectedly like a person who had given up on life. He did not answer, he did not even seem to register that they were there. Gary moved towards him.

'Be careful,' Edward warned as he followed behind Gary at a safe distance. The man was wearing khaki shorts and a shirt, his sandals were made of rubber. 'Are you vaHove?' Gary asked again angrily.

'Ye...e...s.s.' It was a slow reply that sounded like an admission of guilt. The man stopped, his hands hung loosely before him. His scalp was clean shaven and he had a long black beard.

'Why did you do it?' Gary advanced like a policeman approaching a law offender. He carried his lanky frame slowly and looked the man in the face.

'She was in terrible pain ... It hurt me to see her suffer so ... and I ... eh ... you know what I did?' The words came slowly and with difficulty.

Gary groaned and pounced. His hands at vaHove's neck. The older man did not move. Gary squeezed and the older man did nothing. Suddenly, Edward threw down his notebook and joined in the assault, punching the older man with a flurry of jabs to the stomach, chest and face. He was beside himself. VaHove fell slowly to the ground. Still Edward did not stop, he gave a vicious kick with his booted foot aiming at the older man's face. VaHove groaned, stretched out his arms and lay still on his back. Blood spurted from his nose and mouth.

'Edward, you will kill him ... stop it!' Theresa shouted hysterically pulling at Edward, while Cathy grabbed Gary who looked as if he was going to continue the attack. 'Stop it!' she shouted at the top of her voice. Everyone seemed to have forgotten Masimba.

The two men stepped back cursing.

VaHove lay still on the ground. His nose was bleeding, his beard was covered with dirt, his bald head from which a trickle of blood oozed, bore the imprint of a shoe.

Everyone gazed stunned at the rapidity with which the situation had changed, and at the silent figure before them.

Then slowly, and with difficulty, vaHove sat up.

'I have already sent for the police and the headman,' he said, 'I deserve punishment.' He spat blood.

'We will wait for the police,' Edward mumbled as if realising for the first time that he had taken the law into his own hands.

'I have nothing to be ashamed of.' Gary broke away from Cathy's restraining hand. Fresh tears trickled from his eyes and he cried, 'That man deserves capital punishment.'

'Gary, leave that to the law.' Theresa came to Cathy's assistance. They walked Gary over to where Edward sat against the wall of the hut, chewing his lower lip and still panting slightly. His notebook open in his hand.

Masimba stood silently at the door of the hut, holding up his oversize trousers with his left hand.

'Gary, sit down,' Cathy appealed.

'It is not over yet ... the rapist ... the murderer...' The women pressed the younger man down.

Masimba stared silently at them both.

'These children need our protection ...' Gary's voice was no longer angry. 'I hope the police will be here soon.'

Theresa looked at her watch. 'I will take Masimba back to the car.' Nobody replied but their silence gave consent. Cathy led Masimba away, her hand on his shoulders.

'You know, with our police force ... they will not have transport. Cathy accompany the driver to the police station.' Edward said.

Theresa sat down beside the two men.

'We will wait,' Edward closed his notebook.

# My Sekai

I was born Sekai Julius
both names were mine
Shona and English
side by side
I cherished them
for they named me
I called them
Sekai Julius
I heard them
call me
Sekai Julius
I listened to them
Sekai Julius
But my people
stopped calling me Sekai
stopped calling my name
took Sekai away from me.

I am Sekai Julius
Julius makes Sekai
Sekai makes Julius
both names that
make me.

# Colour blind

He leaned against the bar
drank his beer
from a jar
gave wild burps
and joked with his mistress
that God
is a white-bearded individual
a colour-blind old man
who does not know
the colour
of the man he created
in the hotbed
of Africa.

# The Accident

The outside is overcast
with murmurings and mutterings
that it was the work
of private service officers
who pushed the victim's car
in the path
of an oncoming army truck
to cause an accident
that took place
on the front page
of the Daily Tribune.
A bullet wound
was found
below the neck
when a post-mortem
was demanded
by relatives of the deceased.

# The African sun

The African Sun
shines bright
even upon dictators
warms even
absolute rulers,

Sets even upon despots.

# 2

# 'Are we together?'

The previous two weeks had been very cold and windy but on Sunday the sun shone. I smiled as I drew the curtains on the small window of my one rented room. It was warm and balmy outside. I whistled my favourite Sungura tune as I went to queue for the bathroom and the laundry sink. One had to be in the queue before dawn in order to bathe and avoid being late for work. But today was Sunday and there was no hurry.

I was a lodger in a ten-roomed house in the high density suburb of Chinseri, sharing the homestead with eight other families. Today the queues were short. I was number three in the bathroom queue and number four in the laundry queue. I indicated my presence in each queue by placing my red plastic tins in the line of buckets and dishes that had already formed before the laundry sink and the bathroom. Someone was already bathing. She was religious in song and happy to be showering on such a pleasant day; happy not to be late for whatever she intended to do. The bathroom was a known source of disputes because some residents shamelessly jumped the queue. Others deliberately took too long, or were naturally slow. Both types were nicknamed 'Samanyanga', elephants.

I would have preferred to bath after doing my laundry – sweat, and then bath. I was still single and my every task was personal. All the other lodgers knew that I never attempted to jump the queue and did not have much laundry. I did not enjoy the luxury of changing my clothes before the dirt was conspicuous. Every Sunday I washed two pairs of Safari suits, two shirts and two pairs of trousers, socks and underpants.

I went round the house to the front, which faced the main tarred road, where the male lodgers sat basking in the sun, enjoying the warmth. Sunday was a day of rest, so the men assembled to chat about football, the weather, politics and current affairs, always concluding with the deteriorating situation in the country. I enjoyed the discussions. No holds were barred,  but the volume of our voices never rose too high.

Occasionally a 'bomb' or a 'straight' would be shared, and one or two twists of mbanje smoked but they were not essential. A crate of opaque beer… comrade-ship was what we enjoyed and we felt sorry for the one or two men who stuck to their wives and remained indoors. These meetings livened up my Sundays.

Then the militias came. They arrived from nowhere, ambushed us and trampled on the only flowers in our front garden. They must have moved quietly because we only noticed them when they'd reached our flower-bed. They were wearing party berets: green, yellow, black and red – five men and a woman marching in single file. Their white T-shirts were emblazoned with the picture of a formidable man holding a rifle. They seemed to be too determined to consider politeness.

'Guys, we're here to tell you to come to a meeting at 10 a.m. today at the open ground next to Runyararo Beer Garden,' the leader announced, his eyes fixed on our crate of opaque beer. He swallowed. No one replied. He stood menacingly before us. We avoided looking at him. We knew their tactics. The militias thrived on intimidation, threats and gang warfare. No one volunteered to be our spokesman through fear or because there was nothing really to say.

I raised a scud slowly to my mouth. It covered my face. I drank very slowly and deliberately.

'This is not an invitation that you are free to ignore. We said 10 o'clock, we mean

10 o'clock.' The woman broke the silence as she paged through an old A4 exercise book as if she was looking for our names between its tattered pages. I could see the men watching me greedily as I slowly drank my beer. One, who was carrying an axe handle, paced about. Three others holding bicycle chains stood behind the woman standing in the flower bed. These militias regarded themselves as party youth though they were all about thirty. It seemed the real youths, meaning young-sters, did not enjoy such duties.

'Are we together, guys?' The leader smiled and sounded friendly. He stretched out his hand to take the scud from me but I passed it to Baba vaMati who was sit-ting next to me. I did not look up for a while.

'You guys do not offer ... Give me...' He dropped his hands and left his sen-tence unfinished, disappointment all over his face. He did not like what I had done. I should have given him the scud. His lips moved a little. He seemed about to pro-nounce judgement. We deserved a thorough hiding for refusing to offer him beer.

'We give ... we share and ...?' Baba vaShamiso could not find the words to bail us out, so he handed the militia a full new scud, an apologetic expression on his face. The leader of the militias was happy. He received the scud as if he'd been receiving the sacrament, with two open palms. 'Are we together?' His voice was jovial. He rejoiced at the beer but we did not know what his words meant. He sound-ed like a lecturer trying to capture the attention of his students. He bowed and shook the scud with exaggerated vigour. 'Are we together?' he said again, with-out looking at us. I almost laughed but I knew it was not permissible to laugh at a militia, so I coughed instead. Baba vaShamiso shook his head slowly and smiled. Baba vaChengetai hid his face in the scud.

Are-we-together guzzled his beer lasciviously and when he paused he gave a contented burp accompanied by a gratified click of the tongue. He caught his breath and handed the scud to the woman, who took a long swig in a short moment. Her gullet was large and she seemed well practised. The three other men laid down their arms in preparation for the consumption of beer. The business of comman-deering people to the meeting was temporarily ignored.

'The situation requires that you attend meetings. We are here to inform you to do so.' Are-we-together brushed his lips with the back of his hand. He continued, 'The enemy is after our country. You are aware of what the British and the

17

Americans are doing ...'

'Yes. Yes. Yes.' I stopped his little address, and hurried to agree with him.

'Sure, the British Prime Minister...' Baba vaMatilda joined in, also anxious to interrupt his speech.

'The land issue...'. Baba vaChengetai handed him the butt of a cigarette, which he hastily took to his mouth.

'Like they did to Iraq...' Baba vaShamiso did not want to be left out of the game of silencing the militia who seemed bent on politicising us.

'Let's proceed, Comrades,' the woman said, much to our relief, and she turned and marched away. Are-we-together did not seem to approve.

'You,' he addressed her back. 'Do not give us instructions. Are we together?' He warned and moved towards her, jolting a lanky comrade who was still drinking noisily from the dregs of the scud.

Snatching the container, he up-ended it in his mouth, which seemed more for show than for alcohol, then returned the scud to the woman. It was empty. She peered inside, shook it and slowly put into the crate. She made a loud sharp sound with her tongue.

'Why do you love beer like men?' Are-we-together laughed insultingly. The woman stalked off unconcerned, accustomed as she was to derogatory behaviour.

'Are we together, guys? ... you can bring your beer to the meeting, I do not mind.'

We exchanged heavy sighs of relief as the militias trooped off, our eyes following them until they were behind the hibiscus hedge next door.

'I am not attending the meeting,' Baba vaShamiso declared. He rose and stretched his hands several times, punching the air as if he was preparing for a fight. I knew that despite his baby-face, he was unforgiving towards people who'd annoyed him. A vegetable vendor, he constantly ran the risk of being arrested for illegal vending.

'We are down minus one scud ... those bloodsuckers ... who reap where they did not sow.' It felt like a warned and cautioned statement. The Rastafarian father of Matilda was a commuter omnibus tout. His thirteen units at A-Level and a book-keeping certificate were wasted at Mbare Msika bus terminus.

'Yo...you will have to be, have to be gggggood at sloga-sloganeering, Kelvin.'

Baba vaChengetai perfected his deliberate stammer. He smiled the hopeless smile of an annoyed suburban resident who did not know how to deal with the militias. 'The stadium is no place to go,' he concluded, lifting his hand for another scud. But the atmosphere was subdued, and we were not in a hurry to finish our depleted stock.

'I'm going to the meeting,' I announced, grinning. My friends suddenly all appeared older than me because they had assumed the responsibility of taking care of wives and children whether by desire or by accident. Most of these young fathers brought their offspring to the porch. Sunday morning was valued time, which they spent with their families. Not one of them was older than twenty-three and each had a baby no older than nine months. I was just twenty-two and on a Bachelor of Education attachment programme at a local secondary school. Most of their wives had also done their A-levels and got good grades, with the exception of Mai Shamiso who could not afford to go to upper fifth. She met Douglas, Baba vaShamiso, when she was selling tomatoes at Mbare Msika.

'I am teaching my Shamiso to disassociate ... I mean, to distance herself from ruling parties ... in fact I am grooming her to dislike politics,' Douglas said as he sat down. He had avoided my statement of intent. I wondered how little Shamiso received this grooming at the tender age of eight months.

'Let's drink our beer before those suckers decide to come back,' the Rastafarian said as he tied his long dreadlocks behind his head. He took a scud, drank its contents and placed the empty back in the crate.

'We can buy some more.' Kelvin shook a scud, and quickly unscrewed it. After a long gulp, he observed, 'They have destroyed the only flower-bed.' In reality, it had never really been a bed, or one that contained flowers, but there had been various species of vegetation struggling to survive in soil rather than hard-baked earth.

'The chairman's speech said it all,' I continued, realising that they were not taking my declaration seriously. 'He unleashed these militias on the povo to beat us up. He told the youths to start campaigning right away. His voice was stern. I know what that means. Beat up the people until they submit,' I explained, avoiding eye contact with my friends.

'Comrade Hondo Yapera, tell us, how will you benefit from associating yourself with people like those?' Douglas said and laughed.

'I guess you want to become a treasurer .... because there is really nothing of substance you can join them for,' added Kelvin. They laughed again. Douglas wiped his moustache with his palm.

'But remember ... you teachers are not trusted by the politicians ...' he said. The warning pricked my conscience.

'So, that's a good enough reason for attending the meetings,' I said, 'to exonerate myself.' But Kelvin thought otherwise.

'What crime have you committed?' he asked, passing me a scud.

'Let him go ... it's one mouth less,' Baba vaMatilda sounded smug as he rubbed his palms against each other. 'Perhaps he'll bring us good news.'

'Isn't it about time you left, Comrade Hondo. You've only ten minutes to go before you start chanting.'

'You'll need a lot of beer, a lot of energy to manage those Kongonya dances.' Douglas and Kelvin clapped their hands like amused street kids as I took a swig, enjoying their banter, but feeling uneasy. These were difficult times.

Thirty minutes later I was standing in the large open area near the Runyararo Beer Garden. Hands tucked in my pockets, I stood alone and I felt lonely. The meeting had not yet started and no officials were in sight, though it was already half past ten.

The venue was an open space of ground, that had once been a park. Remnants of a lawn were still visible and a few stunted exotic trees struggled to survive. No one had tended it for years. Litter abounded. It was an area now mainly used for political rallies. The municipal council only sat up to take notice when something catastrophic happened there. The last time the grass had been irrigated was when a drunk, who'd been knifed, was found bleeding on the ground. Half a dozen women sat chanting below a tree beside a broken bench. A durawall surrounded a beer garden to the right and the juke-box blared music for the entertainment of the drinkers. I felt drawn towards the noise. Are-we-together and his comrades stood at the counter sharing a scud. They had situated themselves strategically so as to keep an eye on everyone who came to the counter. I bought myself a pint.

'Are you not buying us one as well?' Are-we-together asked pointedly.

'When you've finished that one.' I said bravely pointing at the scud being nursed by the militia woman.

Are-we-together snatched the scud away from the woman and poured the contents down his throat. He then handed the empty scud to the militia wearing a chain round his waist. Irked, the latter said irritably, 'Why bother passing it to me when you know it's empty?'

'I am the boss here.'

'But I am not your messenger.' They faced one another angrily, then the man with the chain shrugged and turned back to the counter.

I hurriedly paid for a scud in addition to my pint of clear beer and moved quickly away from the militias. I knew that next I would be ordered to buy them cigarettes.

Nursing my own beer, I observed them from the other side of the juke-box.

Downing the scud that I had bought, they marched out of the beer garden. People reluctantly started to filter out after them. A few rickety benches had been pulled to the front of the park area, and the militias immediately occupied them. They were joined by two women and a man who had not been with them in the beer garden. We sat on the ground facing them. The meeting began.

'Forward with the party! *Pamberi!* Forward with the repossession of our land! *Pamberi!* Down with the opposition! *Pasi!*' The fifty-strong crowd chanted in response to every slogan as the female militia wearing a party scarf stood at the front and screamed the slogans at us. She raised her right fist and punched the air. ... *Pamberi!* ... *Pasi!* She was not going to stop until she'd worked us up to fever pitch. Very light in complexion, her mouth and eyes were too close to her nose, and her metallic voice was full of hate.

'My name is Comrade Mabhunu. Forward with the party! Forward with repossession of the land! Down with the opposition!' We thundered in response with fists punching the air.

'We now ask Comrade Mambara to lead us in prayer. Forward with the party! Forward with repossession of our land! Down with the opposition!' We responded with vigour. Reluctant cadres would be too quickly noticed. We knew the consequences.

'Forward with the party! *Pamberi!* Forward with the repossession of our land! *Hondo yeminda!* Down with the opposition!' *PASI!* Mambara shouted and bowed his head. He did not give us the chance to respond. He was in a hurry to consult the Almighty. His voice was as hoarse. 'Lord, God of men, who created the world. We pray that with your kindness you will hear us when we pray. We beseech you to kill the leader of the opposition for us. We will be most grateful if you will grant our request. Please, Lord, give us your favourable consideration.' I did not join in the chorus of Amens.

'Forward with the repossession of our land! Forward with the party! Down with sell-outs!' He sat down before we responded.

The political commissar rose again. She repeated her slogans again. 'Forward with the party! Forward with the repossession of our land! Down with the opposition! We now call upon the chairman, Comrade Savage, to address us.' She waited for our responses. Her eyes scanning the crowd for reprobates who failed to chant her slogans or chant them loudly enough.

Are-we-together stood up and took a swig of beer. 'Forward with the party! Down with opposition! We cannot address this meeting as we intended, because the people in this area have failed to attend. So I declare this meeting closed. *Pamberi nehondo yeminda! Pasi nevatengesi!* Have I made myself clear! *Pasi nevatengesi.'* He was brief, but we understood the message too well. 'We will be back next week.' The crowd did not respond but dispersed and disappeared as if it was escaping from a horrible experience.

I walked slowly back home, a beer still in my hand. I felt hot. The slogans rang in my ears. Rang in my head. Seeped into my soul. The metallic voice echoed threateningly. I had made myself more, not less, visible.

I imagined Douglas, Kelvin and the Rastafarian sharing a scud and waiting to hear from me. I did not know what I would say.

# Heroes

Give me
a chisel and a hammer.
I want to cut
on granite
the names of heroes
not buried at Heroes Acre
but interred in shrines
of the people's minds,
men and women
who passed on
at scenes
of specified accidents,
names missing
in classified notices,
unspoken effigies
       on silenced lips.

# The Merc

A metallic blue Mercedes Benz
came to a halt
like an ambulance
at a hospital emergency entrance.
A big man leapt out,
strode to a kiosk
as if he was hurrying
to a pharmacy.
He produced a banknote,
handed it over
as if he was buying
some rare prescribed drug.
The attendant gave him
a toasted cigarette.
He lit it,
puffed a few long drags
and walked slowly back
to his Merc
to convalesce.

# 3

# New Beginnings

**Below a *hozi*,** a granary raised off the ground, you find all sorts of things: hoes, broken clay pots, old gourds, tattered baskets, spent brooms, items that have outlived their time. Chickens roost under the *hozi*, as do lizards, rats, snakes and other crawling creatures. Amai Chido's *hozi*, a pole and *dhaka* house built on a platform of logs that rested in turn on stone pillars, was one of the two rooms which made up her compound. Amai Chido kept all her disused utensils under her *hozi*. She never threw anything away.

Amai Chido, a thin short woman of forty-eight, knelt down and peered cautiously below her granary. There were too many things there. Right now she was looking for a hoe, which she intended to sell or barter for maize and rapoko. She had no food. The *hozi* was empty. She'd swept the floor for rapoko grains only the previous week. The two previous harvests had brought miserable yields.

There, in the darkness, Kutu, a bitch, was suckling four tiny puppies. Amai Chido's fearful face broke into wrinkles of laughter when she looked closer at the bitch and its tiny puppies. Kutu lay on her side flapping her tail to drive away the flies. The bitch's long bony face regarded Amai Chido trustingly and the puppies cuddled against their mother oblivious of their delighted visitor.

'Old lady, another litter. You are filling the whole village with your offspring. Which home does not own one of your brood?' There was pride in Amai Chido's voice. Kutu was her only companion and she always spoke to her freely, sure there was some understanding in the old bitch. She knelt right down to get a better view. The newborn puppies were groping for their mother's teat. 'This is your eighth litter, old lady. Isn't it time you gave up?' Kutu looked at Amai Chido and back at her puppies as if she understood what was being said. 'Who was the father this time?' she asked, touching the puppies. Kutu did not growl. They trusted each other. It was always Amai Chido's privilege to touch the puppies first.

Kutu's puppies looked like little brown foxes, just like Musonza's bulldog. They were quite unlike their mother who had the lean graceful frame of a greyhound.

'*Makorokoto!* Congratulations!' Amai Chido clapped her bony hands, ripples of delight creasing away from her mouth. She squeezed the bitch's hairy neck. '*Makorokoto* to Musonza's dog!' Kutu turned her gaze away from the woman as if in protest that there was no need for such congratulations.

'You can rest now, old lady, and dream away the post-natal blues,' Amai Chido patted Kutu and rose to leave. She laughed again as she glided back to her kitchen, a round pole and *dhaka* hut which faced the *hozi*. She had forgotten about the hoe. She was feeling happy for Kutu.

'But how will I feed your puppies?' The question dropped from her thin lips as she approached the door to the kitchen. The sound of her voice was forlorn. She stood at the door and observed the inside of her kitchen.

The fireplace was full of ash, bits of charcoal and a half-burnt log. Amai Chido was not eager to clean the fireplace and set a new fire. Her situation was not encouraging. She did not have any mealie-meal, vegetables or sweet potatoes with which to cook. Her pots, several still crusted with dried mealie-meal, lay idly beside the cold fireplace. The sun was high but Amai Chido had not made any effort to sweep the kitchen or wash the plates and pots.

The October sun was heating the air. Her surroundings seemed lifeless because most creatures were lying still in some place trying to keep cool. '*Tske.*' Amai Chido swore aloud. The heat of yesteryear had not brought rain, and fear of another drought clouded her mind. She shuddered. How was she going to survive another drought, she thought. She had no seed. How was she going to find food for herself and the dogs? Finding no answer to the questions, she walked hopelessly around the small hut, finally sitting herself down against the wall of the single round room. A dry wind swelled above the thorny shrubs from a gulley beyond her isolated compound, swirled and disappeared into another treeless gulley to the other side. Amai Chido's homestead was perched between these menacing gulleys, isolating it from the rest of the village. She hated gusty winds because she believed they drove away the clouds that were pregnant with rain. 'Again? Another drought?' She talked to herself. She was used to talking to herself because she lived a solitary life. Since Chido, her daughter, had left, Kutu had been her sole companion. The villagers knew her as the woman who was always followed by a bitch. Kutu followed her wherever she went: to the grinding mill, to fetch firewood, to the well, to funerals. At night Kutu drove away intruders, potential rapists and thieves but she was not a hunter. Amai Chido sighed and stretched out her legs.

It was past midday and the sun glared on the devastated terrain. The dry sweat around her neck, chest and armpits made her skin itch. Scratching herself, she remembered the hoe. It was her only hope. Somewhere in the village she would find someone who needed a hoe and had some maize to exchange for it. Some over-zealous farmer with inflated expectations of a rainy season ahead. She removed her dirty doek, and wiped her face and salty neck with it. The veins stood out on her bony forehead. Fanning herself with the faded cloth, she picked over a few villagers whom she thought might feel pity for her. There were several old women who would probably sacrifice one or two buckets of mealie-meal in exchange for the hoe; women with sons working in town who were thus protected from the worst of the drought. She thought of her daughter, Chido, and her mind drifted from town to town. Towns she had never been to but which she knew by name. She sighed.

Chido had set off from the village to Rusape, a small town in the eastern highlands about sixteen kilometres away from her home. Her sole mission had been to seek work, any type of domestic labour. She had left home when she was only eighteen years old. She had wanted to play a pivotal role in the sustenance of their lives. Her widowed mother could do nothing but till the fields whose soil was exhausted and unproductive.

Chido spent three weeks in Rusape and then she sent her mother twenty dollars, writing to inform her that she was proceeding to Mutare where chances of finding employment were greater. Rusape was a small town and her chances of finding work were non-existent. She did not say where she had got the money to send her mother. She wrote again two months later to say Mutare had serious housing problems and to find a job required accommodation. Her vegetable selling venture was failing but still she sent her fifty dollars. The next letter she wrote was from Masvingo. It sounded as if things were at last working out in her favour. Lodgings were plentiful and her vending business was flourishing. The letter was graced with a hundred dollars. Three months later she sent another a hundred dollars. Amai Chido smiled as she remembered the small wad of ten red notes which she collected at the local business centre, which had a mobile postal service. She squinted again into the haze of heat as if some salvation hung in the dry air beyond the veranda. For a while she imagined her daughter doing well. She was happy for her. She observed her cracked feet and her torn dress, now three years old. That letter had been her last contact with her daughter. On several occasions Amai Chido had asked a villager to write letters for her to her daughter but she had not had a reply. Was she still in Masvingo or had she moved on? Her mind drifted away.

She was startled awake by Kutu who appeared from behind her. The bitch was making little whining noises accompanied by weak but desperate gestures which Amai Chido seemed to understand.

'Kutu, get away. *Pfutseke!*' But Kutu stretched her body forward and backwards as if she were waking from a long sleep. Amai Chido was disturbed. She was not in the mood for maternal affairs.

'What do you want? I do not have any food.' She remembered that Kutu had not appeared for supper the previous evening. Although her meal had been too small to share with her old companion there was no doubt that she would definitely have thrown the bitch a morsel. She could not eat while the dog watched her with its huge gentle eyes. Kutu yawned weakly. Her moist teats hung heavily below her hollow ribbed body. It seemed the puppies were sucking her last ounce of flesh.

'You will have to start hunting, old lady,' Amai Chido said with a hopeless chuckle. But Kutu did not go away. Instead, she lay down beside her and slowly closed her eyes. 'You can lie here for as long as you like but I do not know where I can find food for you,' the woman's voice slipped into the dry air like a ghost. Kutu remained asleep. 'You will have to start running around in the bush,' but she grimaced as she observed what remained of the worn land in which hares and mice could not survive. She clapped her hands once resignedly. Kutu woke, glared and closed her eyes again, as if she too had had enough.

'There is nothing I can do either,' Amai Chido shrugged. 'I have always done what I can.' She drew her legs away from Kutu as if she were distancing herself from the dog's plight and closed her eyes. She found sleep but only in momentary doses.

When she awoke, Kutu had gone. She felt dazed. The heat was still oppressive. She held on to the wall of the hut as her thin body lifted itself slowly off the ground. She tied the knot of her doek carelessly, and it seemed too large for her head. She thought of the hoe. She had to find the hoe. She walked across to the *hozi* again. The hoe was her only salvation. It would keep her going, at least for a few days.

Once again she knelt down besid the empty granary, taking care that she did not arouse or disturb the undesirable. She peered into the darkness. The puppies were asleep in a shallow hole under the *hozi*. Kutu was not with them.

'Where have you gone now, old lady?' Amai Chido looked around. 'Kutu!' she called. The puppies stirred blindly. 'Kutu!' she called again. Her voice was loud and urgent. She peered beneath the *hozi* as if she expected the dog to come running out. Kutu never ignored her calls. Where could she have gone? Amai Chido bit her lower lip. Then, seeing a a torn basket lying on its side, she whispered to herself, 'I hate to do this but I cannot bear…' Then she sighed, shrugged and heaving herself forward pulled the basket towards her. She looked around again as if she feared an intruder and did not want to be seen. Then, nervously stretching herself full-length she reached for the puppies and placed them one by one in the basket.

Picking up her cargo, and holding the basket carefully so that the puppies could not drop out, she walked purposefully down the path that led to an anthill, constantly looking over her shoulder lest Kutu see her. The tiny pups made little uncomfortable whimpering sounds as they tried to keep their balance.

There was a large hole at the mouth of the anthill. She looked around her and then threw the basket into the hole. It disappeared into the dark cavity. She turned and hurried back to the compound, breathing heavily. She ran a little, tripping herself when she stepped on the hem of her already torn dress. She looked back again and again as if she expected the puppies to come running after her. She fell to the ground. *'Maiwee!'* The sound of her voice was that of a person not anticipating help. Her voice was too loud. Her throat was dry but there was a lump in it. She lay on her stomach, her legs outstretched and her head fell on her right arm muffling her sniffs as she lay sprawled in the heat. The sun did not spare her.

She thought of the puppies. She thought of Kutu. She thought of the puppies scrabbling in the dark hole. She imagined Kutu searching everywhere for her puppies. She remembered how the puppies lay cuddled next to their mother's teats. She began to sob. Her doek slipped from her head. Sweat and tears flowed down her face. She lay on the ground for a long time, the heat and the emotion had drained all her remaining energy away.

Time passed and slowly a semblance of strength returned to her. She looked up dazed. Her doek lay where it had fallen off her head. Her eyes were red, her lips were dry and cracked. She felt as if she had suffered a bout of fits. She looked back down the path that led down to the anthill and saw Kutu coming up the path carrying one of her puppies between her jaws. It was alive and whimpering. Her face stretched in disbelief as she opened her mouth to say something. Kutu trotted past her towards the *hozi* and in no time she was hurrying back to the anthill, her head down, in a movement of concentrated urgency.

Then through the haze of dust, she thought she saw Chido walking towards the compound, a big cardboard box on her head and a suitcase heavy in her right hand. She blinked in disbelief. Behind Chido she seemed to see two men carrying parcels. Amai Chido blinked in disbelief. As the figures approached she wondered if she was hallucinating. She struggled to her feet.

*'Amai!'* Chido called or was it only the wind in the *hozi*?

# Ode to a tree

Grandad says,
that tall leafy trunk
they call a tree
in a glass case
being exhibited at the show
used to grow everywhere.
You could keep a tree
like a pet, he claims.
I do not believe his words
though he sounds convincing.
He talks of vast forests
where these trees grew.
I fail to imagine
these forests
where wild trees
were sanctuary to animals.
Where have they gone
these mysterious trees,
these forests?
Grandad is crazy
I tell you.
He says he used to climb
to play upon trees
in his father's backyard.
He wants me
to believe that!
Look at this dry land.

31

# *Christmas Day News*

Here is the main news
on this
Christmas Day broadcast.
A total of fifty-two mothers
were blest
with a total of fifty-two babies
born today, Christmas Day,
at our major hospitals,
thirty girls and twenty-two boys
for the first time
in six years
there are no twins.
On a sad note
Christmas Day this year
recorded the highest number
of fatal road accidents
in six years
that have claimed the lives
of seventy-three people.
The figures may rise
when reports from remote parts
of the country are received.

# 4

# Sisters-in-Law

*The two sisters* arrived after their mother had been collected by the undertaker. Their brother had accompanied the body. The sad news had reached the sisters with a phone call early that morning but transport was not readily available. They had hitchhiked sixty kilometres from Chitungwiza to Norton. It was the unfortunate period of fuel shortages.

'Tonderai behaves like a kid – he should have come to collect us in his car.' The older sister complained as she strapped her baby on her back.

'He has stopped thinking for himself, that brother of ours. That woman Tracey does everything for him.'

Arriving at their brother's home, they rang the doorbell once and then strode in. Their brother's wife sat on a stool holding the telephone. Her face wore a vacant stare.

'Why are you not answering the doorbell?'

'How did mother die?' Tracey did not know which question to answer first. The sisters seemed to be angry rather than mourning.

'I am sorry about mother.' Tracey drew their attention to the formalities of consolation, although she still appeared confused.

'Is the doorbell working?'

'How did mother die?' The questions competed aggressively with each other.

'Yes. I am trying to get hold of people …'

'Which people?'

'Relatives — our …' Tracey abruptly ceased to speak.

'Who gave you permission to do so? What qualifies you to do this?'

'Mother died in my arms …' Tracey wanted them to realise that she was carrying a burden, and had been doing so since the tragedy happened. But the two sisters were in no mood to indulge her. She was a daughter-in-law, and thus she must first be given permission — permission from daughters of the deceased — before she could undertake any family obligations.

Tarisai, the younger but larger sister, stood legs astride and hands on hips.

'I … er …' Tracey realised that she was not considered close enough to continue with her self-imposed duties. She replaced the receiver in its cradle, and closed the phone book slowly. The sisters decided to find themselves somewhere to sit and placed themselves squarely on the sofa. There Tarisai helped Shuva to unstrap her baby. They wore cheap black cotton dresses (the colour was fading on the shoulders) and new pairs of black Tommy tennis shoes that they'd brought en route to Norton. Tarisai wore a black beret, military style.

'Why did you not phone us yesterday, when you knew her condition had worsened?'

'Tonderai … said that he was er … going to phone.' She put her hand up to disguise a yawn. Her apparent sleepiness and generally hesitant manner irritated the two sisters even more.

'Just now you were on the phone telling the whole world that you cared for your mother-in-law and now you can't even sit up and talk to us.'

'We haven't had a minute's sleep in the last twenty-four hours. I'm sorry, Auntie.' Tracey wanted them to appreciate the effort that she and their brother had taken in caring for their mother. 'Mother fell ill at supper last evening. She cried out continuously through the night.' The younger woman wanted them to understand that it had been an ordeal, and that they had done their best to attend to the old woman.

'What was she complaining of?'

'Stomach-ache. She vomited several times.'

'But still you and your husband decided not to inform us?' It felt like a declaration of war. The sisters were on an assault mission.

'*Tete*, mother of Tapiwa, you do not know what it was like. You think that it was like this or that … you just think … and that's why you seem to blame us, always blame us.'

She was talking from experience. She had seen her mother-in-law die, in her arms.

Although she had no nursing experience, she had cared for her husband's mother, who had suffered a stroke. She was baptised into married life by taking an invalid mother-in-law into her home when she was a bride of but six months and only twenty-one years old. It had been a long sad honeymoon. Her mother-in-law could hardly move, half her body was paralysed. The days were the most trying because she was alone and her husband was at work. They could not afford to place the sick woman in a nursing home or employ a nurse to look after her. Tracey had depended on common sense, the basis of all good practices: feeding the patient and administering medicines proved simple duties. Bathing and changing soiled clothing were tasks that required two people to help each other. There was no one to help Tracey during the day when her husband, Tonderai, was at work. At times the mother chose not to co-operate. She would lie inert with her eyes closed for hours. The sisters came to visit their mother but they observed a strict two-hour hospital visiting period. They demanded to see their mother being given holistic attention, but they never spared a helping hand, and they never spent the night.

'I must find some rest – get some sleep before people arrive.' Tracey rose and walked slowly to her bedroom. She also wanted to be alone. The sisters were sapping her of the little energy she had left.

'Are you not giving us something to eat?' It was a demand that she could not entertain because she was weak. She realised that in spite of the efforts she put into caring for their mother, the sisters only cared for their rights as guests and daughters of the deceased.

'Help yourself — there is plenty of food in the kitchen,' she said, too tired to care. She fell asleep immediately she laid her head on the pillow.

'What rudeness! How could she display such rudeness to us?' Amai Tapiwa, the elder sister, incited Tarisai with her grievances.

'She is a daughter-in-law. She must prepare a meal for us.' It suited Tarisai to assume a role that was not hers; Tracey was after all her sister-in-law.

'Let's leave her alone for a while,' Shuvai was prepared to wait. 'We will demand a comprehensive post-mortem later,' she said with suitable venom.

'There is much more to the death of our mother than what this girl has told us. She will talk. We will get her to talk.'

'Our brother is now a cabbage. How can Tonderai be so dumb as to leave that wife of his to kill our mother?' Her voice was hard. Tarisai rose. 'Let's prepare ourselves breakfast before the mourners arrive.' She disappeared into the kitchen. Shuvai followed. Their appetite was as keen as their words of incitement; they enjoyed egging each other on. Mourning their mother had become a secondary issue. In the kitchen they feasted. It was their brother's home, their brother's food, after all.

'The lounge must be cleared of all the furniture to make room for the mourners.' Shuvai mopped her face with the baby towel. Sweat from a surfeit of hot food trickled from her nose and chin.

'We can get help from the gardener.' Tarisai concurred. 'Did you see anyone working in the garden when we arrived?'

'No. Maybe he's working at the back of the house.'

With the gardener's help they took all the furniture from the lounge and heaped it on the lawn at the front, spreading the chairs in a circle.

'The men will sit,' they concluded, gratified that they were making the necessary accommodation arrangements for the mourners.

'I think Mukoma Ranganai should stop work. What will the people say when they find the gardener still working on a day of mourning?' Shuvai had made herself comfortable on the porch, little Tapiwa cradled in her arms.

'But he must not leave the premises. He may be required at any time,' Tarisai was in agreement. They enjoyed the freedom of total control.

'Ranganai, tie a red cloth at the gate so the mourners can find their way here,'

Shuvai was not to be outdone by her sister in initiative.

'I have not yet had my breakfast …' Ranganai contained himself, not sure how to behave towards his boss's commanding in-laws.

'You are excused,' the sisters chorused. 'You may go and have your breakfast.' Tarisai eased herself onto a stool and began fanning herself with her hands. 'Where do you stay?'

'At the back. … Is the food ready?' Ranganai asked, pointing towards the kitchen, politely indicating that he took his meals from the big house, and he did not have to go to his own to prepare what he needed.

'They provide you with meals?'

'Yes, breakfast, lunch and supper.' He took two hesitant strides to the door.

'We cannot be sure … we do not know.'

'How much breakfast? Bread, eggs, sausages, bacon, tea, coffee?' Shuvai inquired sarcastically.

'They give me what they eat.' He swung the lounge door open and disappeared inside.

'I think I'll have to follow — to see — how much he takes …' Tarisai rushed after Ranganai.

The August wind whipped the trees but the sun warmed the spring air. The musasa leaves were turning coral pink as the huge trees cast wide shadows over the rest of the garden.

Shuvai laid her child Tapiwa to sleep on a small mat on the porch while she sat on a stool, her hands resting on her knees. Not long afterwards, she rose screaming and ran down the driveway, as she saw her brother's Datsun drive slowly up to the house. 'Where have you put our mother? Where have you sent our mother?' she cried as she ran down the concrete path. Her scream disturbed the peace that was settling over the warmth of the late morning. The baby woke and joined in the fray. Tonderai stopped the car before his sister ran straight into it and hurt herself. He stepped out of the vehicle and watched his sister fall in a frenzy at his feet.

'You will hurt yourself, Amai Tapiwa,' he said calmly.

'Where is Mother?' Her tone was accusing. 'Where have you put our mother?' She grabbed his feet with both her hands and held tight.

'Mother has left us.' Tonderai lifted her up. 'Mother is now resting. She has joined our father beyond.'

Shuvai's scream had summoned Tarisai who did not want to be outdone in her protestations of grief. She gave a piercing scream, which announced to the neighbourhood that something terrible had happened at Tonderai Marufu's residence. Running down the driveway she joined her brother and her sister, whose knees were grazed and bleeding, and ecstatically joined the performance of hopping, jumping and hugging Tonderai.

'She suffered for a long time – she has at last found rest in the Lord.' The man's sensible words were heard by neither sister in their shared hysteria.

An old woman walked up the driveway: a neighbour, she had heard the screams and come to investigate. She was followed by a dog. 'What is it, son?' she asked.

'Mother passed away at dawn today.'

'She should not have left us this way,' wailed Tarisai.

'We are now orphans,' moaned Shuvai.

And they subsided into sniffs and competitively loud sighs.

'I am sorry.' The old woman shook their hands. 'It is the way we will go. All of us.'

'The stroke debilitated her. We did all we could,' Tonderai's face was weary.

'Let us go to the house, my children.' The old woman stretched a frail hand and summoned Shuvai to stand. 'You should be strong at such times. You must accord your mother befitting respect.'

They walked to the house, keeping pace with the old woman. The sisters continued to weep but now that they had the beginnings of an audience they could afford to exercise restraint. Arriving at the house, they all made themselves comfortable on the carpet in the lounge. In the meantime, Tonderai had driven his car round to the back porch and unloaded packages of food for the wake which was expected to last about three days: cabbages, meat, cooking oil and mealie-meal. Sugar and milk would always be available at his local shopping centre. Then he joined his sisters and his neighbour and told them all he could about their mother's last days.

'It was only last night that the situation became really serious. I phoned Tapiwa's father twice on his mobile last night but there was no network. Where is he?'

'He's away at his rural home. I phoned Gambe Stores and asked them to send a message to him. He's gone to Muzarabani. He will certainly come when he gets the message,' Shuvai explained.

'Where is Tracey?'

'Asleep. Some of us can sleep without shame even in these grievous times.' Tarisai never missed an opportunity to cast aspersions on her sister-in-law.

'She did not even have the courtesy to explain – as you have done – what really transpired.' Shuvai's voice was low but emphatic.

'She did not sleep last night. She was with mother throughout. We had quite a bad time.' The sisters looked at each other in disbelief. How could their brother express appreciation of his wife's efforts? They despised him.

'She is the mother now in this homestead. She has a duty to welcome the mourners,' Tarisai said with contempt.

'My children, this is not time for ... I should think you should be grateful that your sister-in-law took care of your mother until her death, and thank your brother for all his efforts in looking after her. Right now you should sit down and make funeral arrangements.' The old woman's small fist thumped her left palm as she talked. She had the advantage of age. The sisters did not deign to answer.

'Let her rest a while. ...Ranga!' Tonderai stood up.

Ranga appeared. His mouth was full of bread. 'You are having breakfast – why so late?' Ranga did not reply. 'OK, when you're through, please put all the food in the pantry. After that, find the keys to the storeroom and bring out all the chairs and tables for the mourners. And, by the way, all that furniture heaped on the lawn is being damaged by the sun. Tracey will not want her furniture spoiled. Find someone to help you move it somewhere safe. We will also need firewood. There is plenty at the back in the yard. I will pay whoever you get to help you – but eat first.' Tonderai went out to the garden and found himself a secluded cool place to rest. In no time he was asleep.

Tracey awoke. She heard women singing solemn funeral songs to the accompaniment of a drum and rattles. She could tell from the wailing that groups of people were arriving as they brought variations to the sound of crying. She could also hear bursts of laughter which came from behind the house. She realised that some women had started cooking. She got off the bed, bathed, changed her clothes, applied a little make-up and went down to the kitchen to find something to eat. Tarisai, who'd been keeping an observant eye open for her sister-in-law got up from the lounge floor and went into the kitchen.

'Good afternoon *Tete*, please join me.' Tracey said as she rose from her chair to get a cup from the kitchen unit.

'No. I am not in the mood for food. How can I be when my mother is in the undertaker's mortuary?' Tarisai stood akimbo before Tracey.

'You do not have to starve yourself, *Tete*. Death is our way — our end,' Tracey said gently, hoping to console her sister-in-law, unaware that she was fanning a fire. She returned to her seat. 'Mother is resting — she suffered and she is now at peace.'

'So you wanted my mother to die. You were tired of nursing her. You wished she were dead.' Tarisai pointed at her sister-in-law with her thick finger.

'No, *Tete*, of course not, but you must know how much she was suffering ...'

'I should know what!? You are now happy ... celebrating. You are feasting and you have dressed up for the occasion that you desired.'

'*Tete?* How can you?' Tracey felt out of her depth before such hostility and aggression.

'I know. You are just putting on a show — pretending that you are saddened by the death of our mother.' Spittle formed at the corner of Tarisai's mouth.

Tracey slowly put down her cup. She could not understand these accusations. She was not aware of having crossed swords with her in-laws, and had always accorded them due respect.

'I will not have my mother buried until a full inquiry has been conducted — a comprehensive post-mortem.'

'Are you suggesting that mother's death was caused by us,' Tracey paled, stood up and poured the remains of tea into the kitchen sink. Quietly she put away the loaf of bread and cleaned the table. She was waiting to hear what further accusations her sister-in-law would level against her.

'Not my brother — how could he kill — murder his mother?' She took a step towards Tracey who watched her every movement. 'You are going to talk.' It was a threat, and with that she turned her back and went into the lounge. Tracey sat heavily down on the chair and began to cry.

Not long afterwards Tonderai found his wife crying alone in the kitchen. 'Tracey, do not take mother's death too hard. You always did your best.' He rubbed her shoulders gently. He knew that his wife and his mother had accepted each other's positions with mutual affection since he had first introduced them, and they had enjoyed each other's company. 'She suffered and the Lord has taken her to her resting place.' His voice broke. Tracey rose quickly and embraced him. For the first time since their mother's death, he wept.

'There were times,' he said, 'when I wished the Lord would take her. I hated her helplessness and the demands that it made on you. It hurt me.' Regret and exhaustion compounded his grief.

Tarisai emerged and stood at the kitchen door. Seeing two people entwined in an embrace, she retreated fast. Tonderai saw her but Tracey did not and she did not mention his sister's accusations and hostility. She pitied her husband who was grieving alone.

Meanwhile the mourners increased. The singing grew louder.

Husband and wife parted. There was still much to be done. Tonderai went to help Ranganai kindle a fire for the male mourners. Tracey made her way to the yard at the back of the house. She was anxious to meet the women who were preparing to do the cooking, and help them with provisions. Then, having done all she could, she moved into the lounge where the female mourners were sitting on the floor singing. Her phone began to ring. Tarisai and Shuvai gazed at her furiously, as if to say, you only had to arrive to spoil the atmosphere. Tracey, who had barely sat down, rose, hand in her pocket, and hastily left the room walking quickly towards the garage where no one could be disturbed. Tarisai's stare followed her out of the porch door. She leant against the car and answered the call, oblivious that Tarisai had followed her.

'She passed away early this morning ...' but before she could say any more, Tarisai grabbed the phone and switched it off.

'How dare you make phone calls! You are not even sorry that... that your husband's mother is dead! What kind of person are you?' Tarisai shouted, clenching her fists as if she was ready to fight.

'It's my people, my father. He wants to know where the mourners are gathered.' Tracey spoke slowly, restraining her reactions, while her heart beat furiously. She twisted her hands behind her back.

'I do not care who it is or who it was...' Tarisai said, putting the phone between her ample breasts. 'I will keep this. You haven't settled to mourn with us for even a minute. Have you no heart! This phone is now mine!'

'Please – give me back my phone, *Tete*.' Tracey stretched out her right hand to receive it.

'*Aiwa!*' Tarisai laughed.

Tracey's equanimity vanished. She lunged forward and grabbed her by the throat with both hands. Tarisai was caught unawares and fell backwards. Tracey fell on top of her. And then, realising her advantage, sat up legs astride her sister-in-law. Tarisai uttered a few groggy sounds of complaint, kicking the air with her new tennis shoes.

Tracey retrieved her phone, rose, drew back and stood ready to retaliate if Tarisai became offensive. Tarisai held her throat with both hands. 'Kill me. Kill me too ...' she moaned.

Shuvai appeared singing a lullaby, her child on her back. Unaware that she was moving into a battlefield, she was trying to soothe her baby to sleep, away from the mourners. Startled to see her sister lying on the ground, and Tracey standing like a wrestler ready to pounce, she gasped, 'Tarisai, whatever is – e – e – e going on?' It was evident that a fight had taken place and her sister had lost.

'Kill me ... like ...' Tarisai cried.

'If you come near me, I'll soon forget that you're Tonderai's sister.' Tracey stood her ground, like an impala defending her young. Shuvai was too surprised to utter, and like all bullies found it difficult to respond when the victim hit back.  She made a swift about-turn and hurried away to call Tonderai. The child on her back whimpered in distress, and the echoes of a mournful dirge came from the house.

Tonderai came running. His gentle, patient wife could surely not be fighting. What could have provoked her? He was not unaware of his sisters' resentment, though like most men, chose to feign ignorance. He put his hands on Tracey's shoulders. She was shaking. 'Tarisai ... is too ... I ... er ... could not stand ... we had a fight.'

Shuvai hurried over to her sister, who still lay on the ground groaning intermittently.

'Tarisai, get up. What did she do to you?''

Let her kill me. The murderer.' Tarisai rose slowly and with as much dignity as she could muster.

She picked up her beret, which had fallen on the ground. 'I'm leaving. But I'll not let this matter rest.'

His sister's words told Tonderai that matters had gone further than he imagined. He opened the rear door of the car, and gently pushed his wife inside. Then he said, 'Tarisai, what happened? Why were you fighting with my wife?'

Shuvai responded aggressively. 'Your wife beat up your sister. What else is there to explain?'

'Why – Tarisai?' Tonderai asked again, looking her in the face. 'Did I hear you call my wife a murderer?' The woman didn't respond. She looked away but made no effort to leave.

'Tell him why,' Shuvai insisted. 'That woman ... .' Tarisai shook her body vigorously like a big hen after a sexual encounter. She turned her head from left to right several times, beat her dusty beret against her thigh and coughed a little. Her brother and sister watched her every movement, anticipating a hysterical monologue. Shuvai moved over to her sister and began dry-cleaning her with Tapiwa's towel. She buttoned her dress at the chest.

'I have come to mourn my mother ... ' She was slow and sounded determined. 'Leave me alone ... I am going into the house. I owe my mother some respect – unlike others.' She pressed her beret onto her head, not in the previous military style but covering her whole crown and ears, and proceeded slowly back to the lounge followed by Shuvai.

Tonderai shook his head resignedly. He remembered their childhood days when he did not stand a chance whenever fights and arguments took place. He was the baby. He could not challenge his sisters. He never won.

Funerals were often a battleground.

# Untitled

He died in exile
in a faraway foreign land.
The news reached home,
his own assembled
to mourn their son
to arrange for
the repatriation of his body
from the land far-away
for a decent burial
back home.
They had no money
to collect the body
of their own
from that foreign land.
They had no money
to send  their own
to bury their own
in the land far away.
As they sat
around ashen fires
in the bereaved yard
they wished
the pauper's burial
of their own
in the faraway land
was decent enough
not to appear
on prime time news
hour.

# If it's not ...

If it's not inflation
it is corruption.
If it's not bribery
it is robbery.
> Confusion flourishes.

If it's not rape
it is murder.
If it's not genocide
it is AIDS.
> Panic thrives.

If it's not nepotism
it is dictatorship.
If it's not Bokassa
it is Amin.
> Skeletons survive.

If it's not a cyclone
it is drought
If it's not the west
it is the east.
> Disaster sets.

Africa!
When will all this end?

# I do love, I do

*I drown myself*
*in the current of my sweat.*
*I hold on*
*to the last thread of my strength*
*for your love.*
*I lose myself*
*in the mist of my breath*
*serving the master*
*to save my love*
*from crumbling like*
*ash without smoke,*
*smoke without a shadow.*
*I do love, I do*
*to save my love*
*from dying out*
*like the severed smile*
*of an imbecile.*

# Subjects

From my bedroom window
I watch them
walk down the road
they pretend
they are not subjects
of a despot
they saunter

      sway

      laugh

      jog

down the street
as if they've had
a square meal
as if they can enjoy
the sunshine
they will not let
the world know
for fear of their skin
yet their ordeal still smells
like a subdued fart.

# Some people

Some people
are full stops, bus stops
that end journeys.
Some people
are commas, sojourns
on the way.
Others are question marks
who thrive on asking
'Where to now, man?'

# 5

## Amai Takawira

**When I arrived** at Joel's place of residence, a few panes of the window to his room were broken. Splinters of glass lay everywhere. Several stones that had been employed to execute the job lay amongst the glass. The string holding the curtain in place was loose, and the window was half open, though the broken panes were letting in enough air. I felt a strong urge to do an about-turn and make for home, but paused to observe the yard. Silence prevailed. His landlady was single, middle-aged and a workaholic, so I did not expect to find her at home. I was accustomed to being welcomed by Joel's CD-player blaring out Sungura, the landlady's favourite music, but there was only silence.

I peered fearfully through the window, and on the opposite wall of his room I saw bloody finger and palm prints. I imagined they were Joel's. The wooden push-tray lay on its side with a leg broken off. The two-plate stove was upside down on the floor attached to a cable without a plug. Water, glass and soil were scattered all over the polished red floor. The large mirror in the middle of the wardrobe was broken,

49

the door hung half open and the cupboard was denuded of clothes. Hangers lay scattered on the floor. The drawers had been pulled open: clothes, shoes, socks, a tube of toothpaste and a toothbrush were all jumbled up as if they been stirred by a madman. A box of condoms had fallen off a shelf and spilled its contents of small blue packets at the front of the wardrobe. Two skirts, a black one and yellow one, were tossed among the male paraphernalia. I concluded they belonged to Mabel, Joel's long-time girlfriend. The palm prints on the wall were too large to have been Mabel's.

Joel's favourite grey tracksuit was covered in blood next to the broken tumblers on the floor. Plates, pots, cups, basins, spoons occupied the most unusual places: some were on the bed and others were under it. The CD-player was intact but sitting on the dressing table, whicht was tilting over on three legs. I could not tell whether the damage was the result of a fight between two or more people or the work of Joel on the rampage, though the latter seemed unlikely given the blood.

I heard hurrying footsteps behind me. Turning my head abruptly and with a sense of fear, I saw Joel's brother walking fast towards me as if he was on a mission to apprehend anyone sneaking in through his brother's window. But he looked tired. I watched him approach me.

'Sekai, whatever has happened?' He licked his dry lips with his tongue and stood breathless before me. He did not sound aggrieved. He just wanted to know.

'I don't know.' I said briefly.

'What's got into him?' He moved next to me, beside the window, but seemed in no hurry to peer inside. He looked at me as if Joel being my friend, I would be able to shed some light on whatever catastrophe had reached his ears. 'It has to be all that mbanje smoking,' he muttered, preparing himself to look through the window.

'No, brother Tongai,' I answered carefully. 'Joel had stopped – we had stopped smoking …' I had, however, noticed a packet full of mbanje under the bed. I hoped Tongai wouldn't notice it. I moved away from the window, hoping he would follow me.

'Have you any idea where he is?' I asked.

'I don't know ….' He did not appear to believe that my question was genuine, and seemed to have run short of words. He looked at me with suspicion.

'His room is in a terrible mess,' I continued, 'and there is blood everywhere.'

'Yes,' he answered, 'someone told me – that he'd seen Joel covered in blood, and that's why I came here as quickly as I could.'

'Gilbert shouted the news from a commuter omnibus thirty minutes ago — I came over immediately. I was on my way back from church.' I wanted to remind him that I was a Born-again Christian.

'Oh?' he said, 'which church?' It seemed to me that he thought I was lying.

'I belong to the Catholic youth club.' I was surprised that I should be anxious that he believe me.

'I believe you,' he responded as if reading my mind. He bit his lower lip, and scratched his chin. I gazed at him in disbelief. He was not behaving like the Tongai I knew. He was not known to maintain his calm when his brother behaved badly. He did not brook rowdy behaviour. He hadn't even mentioned the chaos in the room or the disturbing signs of blood. It seemed to me that someone had been hurt, and hurt badly. I was rescued from further questions by the landlady walking in through the gate.

'Afternoon, Sekai!' She said quickly, though her weariness showed.

'Good afternoon, Amai Takawira! I am sorry ....'

'Good afternoon, Amai Takawira! I'm very sorry about the behaviour of these guys.' Tongai's words raced ahead of mine, as if we were participating in a competition. He talked very fast and he did not sound sorry at all.

'It can be sorted out.' Her manner was detached, and she began walking towards the front door as if whatever had transpired was a matter of indifference to her. She appeared very small but not irresolute.

'If there is anything you wish me to do, please do not hesitate to tell me.' Tongai said to her retreating back. Her hair was tied carelessly behind her head.

'Don't worry. I will sort things out,' she answered, still walking away from us. Then turning briefly, and staring at the two of us still standing by the window, she said firmly,'Sekai, come along with me. I would like to talk to you.' I ran to catch her up, leaving Tongail standing and looking awkward.

'Sekai must tell you what they've been up to. Look at the damage!' Amai Takawira continued to the door without turning. She was humming a Sungura tune. Tongai shouted, 'He must talk!' I swore silently to myself. One day I would deal with him.

'Have you seen Joel?' Amai Takawira asked.

'No — no — I only heard about this a few minutes ago ... someone shouted from the bus and I came over right away.'

'If you see him, you'll feel sorry for him, because he's a mess.' She looked at me, shaking her head. I did not know what to say. I suspected he'd been hurt, and hurt badly because of all the blood. Nonetheless fighting was not new to him and I did not know how she felt about the damage to her window panes. I did not want to say the wrong thing. I did not know what had happened and I did not want to speculate as I felt I would then be implicated.

'Where is he?' I asked. She unlocked her own door and walked into the lounge. I hesitated on the threshold of the room.

'He's been admitted to Chitungwiza Hospital. Come in, Sekai.' She sat down on a sofa facing the door. I walked in as if I was entering a boxing ring and perched myself on a stool next to the door. I avoided the comfort of the sofa.

'Thank you.' It was the loudest salutation I'd ever given. My manners were refining themselves.

'The first thing I would like us to do is to get rid of all the mbanje in that room.' I looked at her open-mouthed. She spoke so casually I could not believe my ears. 'The police may decide to inspect the damage caused during the fracas. You know this is a police case.' She laughed sheepishly. 'Don't look surprised. I know everything. There is a bag of the stuff below the bed. You'll know where to find it.' I was about to deny all knowledge of the dagga in Joel's room, when she pressed on. 'You'd better do what I'm telling you right away. Bring the packet to me.' She was a small woman, but she knew how to make herself felt.

I rose unashamedly and trudged into Joel's room. I did not want the police to find the weed, but I did not want to give her the mbanje. What if it was a trap? What if she wanted to give the police the dagga as an exhibit?

I entered Joel's room. The door was not locked. I had seen what it looked like from outside, but I was still shocked. The blood on the walls, and the sodden tracksuit looked homicidal. I shuddered. I stood for a bit, shaken, not quite knowing what to do. If I reached for the mbanje under the bed, would I be protecting Joel, or would I be implicating myself? Eventually, bending down, I reached for the packet, trying not to touch anything else, which was difficult among the maelstrom of possessions cast about. I felt an urge to hide the packet somewhere, anywhere that the police could not find it.

Suddenly Amai Takawira was standing at the door.

'Have you picked it?' she asked as she stood at Joel's door watching me. 'Here. Give it to me.' She stretched out her hand.

'What are you going to do with it?'

'Safe-keeping – I know what it means to him.' She gave me an 'I-know-all' smile. Handing her the packet, I felt as if I'd betrayed my friend. I followed her back to the lounge. She held the precious weed, cupped tightly in her right palm. 'Do you want some? We can have some.' I neither accepted or refused. I felt that some of my unasked questions were finding answers. She invited me over to the fowl-run at the back of the house.

We went to a place behind the vegetable garden secluded by trees that was clearly often used. Two steel chairs with cushions faced each other in the shade. The fowl-run had no chickens. It served as a storage place for an assortment of goods. We sat down facing each other.

'How do you like it, big or small?' she asked as she prepared the cigarette, removing the seeds meticulously from the dried shreds of leaves. She placed the seeds in a small tin that was already three quarters full. Her composure did not make me comfortable. I felt like a stranger. Yet, I had met her daily when I came to visit Joel. Greeted her. Joked with her. Shared her moments of emotional stress when her spirits were down or when she was ill. But I had never imagined that she smoked mbanje. Joel had never hinted as much, though I was always surprised that Amai Takawira tolerated the noise of his CD-player.

'A reasonable size.' I felt it would be best to say very little. I did not want to show that I was shocked – and worried. I held my peace and she did the same as we shared the cigarette which she had rolled with the expertise of a pro.

In the silence my mind rehearsed events again and again. It seemed she knew everything about my smoking. She did not find it risky to invite me for a puff and she had known that I would know that there was illicit weed in Joel's room. It was as if we were partners in crime.

She slapped her thigh, and the noise brought me back to earth. 'Let's play some music.' She meant Sungura music and nothing else. She slowly heeled the butt of her spliff and rose to lead the way back into the house. She had played the role of hostess, but suddenly she had also become the mistress of ceremonies. She told me what to do and I did what she told me.

'I hope his CD-player is in one piece.' She grimaced as she hummed a Sungura tune. I could not tell whether she was enjoying herself or not. She fell into the sofa and sat with open legs and outstretched hands. I collected the player from Joel's room. It was still intact.

'Which one would you like?' I asked as I pushed the plug into the wall socket.

'You know, Sekai … you know.' She sounded impatient. I went back to collect the discs from Joel's room. Suddenly I felt an irresistible urge to laugh. I felt I was behaving like a small boy while she sat spread-eagled on the sofa waiting to issue further instructions. She was not amused by my unexpected laughter.

'What's funny? What's so funny, Sekai?' She stood up and regarded me for a moment. I put the box of discs on a coffee table between us and continued to laugh uncontrollably. Incensed, she advanced swiftly towards me and slapped me hard on the face. It had no effect. I was beside myself. I'm a tall man: six foot and broad shouldered; beside me she appeared very small. Nonetheless, she was furious. She could not see the joke, and she made as if to slap me again, but I moved my head just slightly: she missed and crashed onto the coffee table. She shrieked, picked up a wooden ashtray, and threw it at me without taking aim. I laughed louder than ever. How could she miss when she was so close? I was amused. The ashtray shattered a window pane. The noise startled me and brought me back to my senses. I ran out of the house and immediately my excitement evaporated. I stood a distance away from the door and waited to see what would happen next. After a few minutes she emerged, the big black pin that had held her hair back hung loosely above her right ear and she walked with a slight limp. She was wearing a single slipper.

'Sekai — I'm sorry.' Her voice sounded forlorn. Hostility had vanished from her face and she stood at the door as if she was somehow hurt. 'Come back — I'm sorry.' I did not understand her sudden mood swings. I looked at her for a moment, noticing that she was only wearing one slipper, and then I walked away, my head sunk between my shoulders. I could hear her calling after me, until I was out of reach.

That evening at the hospital visiting hour, we were both there and standing apart like hostile sentries. I thought I heard her whisper, 'I really am sorry, Sekai.' Joel must have heard her too because he turned his swollen face towards me and then back at his landlady, who stood silent, as if butter wouldn't melt in her mouth. She held a plastic bag full of fruit, and an envelope with a card, a Get Well card, I assumed.

I learnt that Joel fought a drug peddler that morning over a spliff which he had apparently refused to share with the dealer. They had known each other a long time, but still the dealer had given Joel a thorough beating.

I left before Amai Takawira and walked back home to St Mary's, a suburb of Chitungwiza. I had also nearly involved myself in a fight with Amai Takawira. I did not like to think what the outcome might have been. We were not evenly matched. I decided to keep well away, and did not even visit Joel when he was eventually discharged from hospital. I was trying to abstain from drugs and a meeting with Joel would dent my resolve.

However, one evening, weeks later, I met Amai Takawira walking surefooted towards Huruyadzo Shopping Centre in St Mary's. She held an open umbrella above her head, though it was already dark. I made to avoid her but she saw me and leapt in front of me.

'Hi Sekai. How are you?' she asked, standing right in front of me and blocking my way.

'Fine ... er ... thanks,' I replied and turned quickly to the right, but she would not let me go.

'Sekai. Do come under the umbrella. How can you refuse in this downpour?' She quickly positioned her shade just above my head, stretching her arm upright and trotting to keep up with me. It was not raining. What downpour?

'No – I'm OK,' I spoke angrily but quietly, not wanting to create a scene. I felt very stupid. There was no rain, or a sign of rain. We must look ridiculous. 'It's not raining,' I said curtly, walking faster and faster, as I tried to get away from her without actually running.

'Oh, Sekai? You'll get so wet,' she insisted. She sounded desperate. I heard some girls behind us laugh. I took a sudden right turn, and ran. She did not attempt to follow me because I soon vanished into the darkness where there was no street lighting.

A fortnight later, I met the dealer at Huruyadzo Shopping Centre and he approached me. 'I've got some good stuff,' he said, shaking my hand and smiling disarmingly. He knew I would ask about the fight.

'I don't want any.' I was brief and stern. He stared at me in disbelief. I'd always been a customer he could count on. He sold good stuff and didn't mix it. 'What's wrong? You can pay later.' I had qualified to buy on credit over years of bilateral dealings in this illegal trade. He did not want me to go elsewhere.

'No thank you.' He discreetly placed a twist in my palm but I kept my hand open and it fell on the ground. He bent down and took his star back. 'Why did you fight Joel?' I asked unceremoniously. You cracked his jaws.

He scratched his clean-shaven head that shone in the morning heat. 'Me? Beat Joel?' A likely story. 'He's sleeping with my girl — that landlady of his — and she's a wild cat. Don't I know it!' He sounded resentful. 'You know nothing,' he shook his head. 'Nothing. But I can tell you, I'm not going to be scapegoated again.' He turned on his heel and left me looking after him.

# Englished

*From the father*
*to the foetus*
*in the womb*
*they love English*
*so much that*
*they dream in English*
*they pray in English*
*they think in English.*

*Congratulations for a new baby*
*strange cards strange customs*
*displayed in English*
*decorate their homes*
*their heroes are buried*
*in English*
*see the inscriptions*
*'Rest in Peace'*
*on their tombstones.*

*They are so Englished*
*they hate the English*
*for their Englishness.*

# All is not well

All is not well, son.
Birds fly low.
Jets have taken over.

Fishes hide away
from chasing torpedoes.
Rivers fume
behind huge walls.

Wistful faces of people
wishing they did not
belong to a people
of the tents
in a far away land
remind me of boundaries
that flow blood.

# 6

## Sahwira's Condoms

**When Muchena turned** right into Mutsanai Street in the high-density suburb of St Mary's Chitungwiza, his feet had blistered in his tight gumboots. He moved his walking-stick from hand to hand. The September sun was high and hot. He walked with a slight limp. His right boot was squeezing a corn on his toe. The pinch was hot as his gumboots thudded slowly down a street lined with rows of houses. Houses built by unprofessional hands with rusting iron or plastic sheets over unburnt bricks. The hedge that formed the boundaries to these dwellings had not been trimmed. It encroached over the tarmac of Mutsanai Street and into other yards. Holes in the unplastered walls of some houses suggested that gun warfare was the order of the day. Windows were openings in walls and sealed by cardboard that was removed when it became too hot. Muchena arrived at the open gate of a house with a high durawall. It was the only house that was a permanent structure in the whole street.

He stood and observed the people inside the enclosure. Wincing, he moved his sore foot to ease the pain. No one noticed his presence at the gate. Despite the hot sun, they sat huddled around a fire of logs peeling ash. Hunched in overcoats and jerseys, they talked in hushed voices and wore mournful faces. Three elderly women and two young men stood at a secluded corner of the durawall and conferred amongst themselves.

From the gate he could hear weeping women. Others, tear-drenched, made their way through the front door of the big house standing before him. Muchena stood and watched the mourners, who took no notice of him.

'Chimimba! Chimimba! I have come!' Muchena called, before breaking into a forced roar of laughter that could not survive in the deathly atmosphere. Startled, the mourners cocked their heads and looked towards the gate. Muchena glared at them and then pulled a roguish face, which made them all sit up.

'Chimimba! Chimimba!' The mourners stared at each other in astonishment. How could he show such disrespect? They looked at him suspiciously before exchanging inquiring glances with each other. Muchena laughed and then assumed a sarcastic smile. The young mourners sat edgily on their chairs, the elders reclined back pointedly watching Muchena.

'I have come to mourn your son,' Muchena cleared his voice, his eyes wandering slowly among the mourners, 'but not to do your dirty work'. He shook his head, 'No, indeed not. Not this time.'

The mourners wondered who this man in an undersized khaki shirt, pair of gabardine trousers, and gumboots could be. A heavy overcoat hung from his left arm.

'I will not touch the bodies of your dead again.' Muchena raised his metal walking-stick and shook it. The mourners twisted in their seats, their eyes bulging. They whispered amongst themselves and nodded as if in agreement. 'I am not an undertaker,' Muchena breathed heavily, his toad-like eyes rolled sideways. 'I am tired of washing bodies in diapers. Skeletons.' He spat but no saliva came out of his mouth. He rested his whole frame on his metal stick. Some mourners nodded, some scratched their heads and some assumed set expressions. They whispered doubtfully to each other.

'How many of your sons have I buried since the last rains? Two. The one in the mortuary today is the third.' There was a rumble of mutterings among the mourners.

60

'*Sahwira?*' a mourner uttered in a loud whisper.

'*Sahwira?*'

'*Sahwira.*' '*Sahwira.*' The word was passed around as if in agreement. Their expressions lightened. Their bodies relaxed. 'I told you so,' a bold man asserted, his eyes glowing because he had recognised the *Sahwira* before the others.

Muchena straightened his back. His eyes, like those of a chameleon, were everywhere.

'Get this straight, Chimimba.'

He stood as if he was waiting for the man to come and welcome him into his house. But no one rose to greet him and Muchena did not move towards the mourners to shake hands with them as required by tradition.

Instead he clamped his metal walking-stick under his arm. Then he went through the pockets of his heavy coat. The mourners watched spellbound. Unearthing a blue plastic pack, he tore open the small square packet and held high a rubbery sheath. The mourners unwillingly began to laugh, and as their laughter crescendoed some rose from their seats and clapped their hands. The sombre mood was broken.

Muchena raised his voice, 'Get this straight. Funerals in your family have become as regular as church services.' The mourners seemed not to hear him. They were struggling for composure. They wriggled and hiccupped with suppressed laughter. Muchena grinned. He fitted the tip of his walking-stick into the rubber sheath and stretched it to its full elastic length. Holding his stick high, he approached a group of elders who looked down into the fiery logs but their attention was evident.

Muchena raised his stick above their heads.

'Your children do not heed wise words. This thin sheath is the solution to their sexual appetite. Use condoms.' His words were punctuated with spittle. 'They say this every day: "Use condoms for safe sex."' The mourners stared into the glaring logs. They were thinking of Chimimba's son. They had heard that the young man had died of AIDS, a disease associated with sexual intercourse. An incurable disease that was killing many people. Some of the elders recalled the days when they had been sexually active. A time when they had contracted sexually transmitted diseases. Gonorrhoea. Syphilis. They exchanged sighs. Such diseases had been common in their day. They remembered the epithets they had coined for the STDs:

'Landmines'. 'Flowers'. 'Drop'. Many had flirted with different mistresses but there had been no such thing as AIDS during their years of bachelorhood. Venereal diseases were treated like the common flu. One visit to a doctor was enough. But AIDS? The elders exchanged frightened glances. Their grief was temporarily shelved. Their minds were stuck in reverse gear. Some imagined themselves dead, as they revisited their youth.

'Oiling decomposed bodies and clothing skeletons is one gruesome experience.' Muchena's voice cut into their thoughts.

The mourners moved in their seats but they did not raise their heads. They remained mute, baking from the heat of midday sun above and the glowing embers of the fire below. Muchena continued, 'What have I done to deserve such a life? Is it because I accepted your gourd of beer, the meat of your fat goat on the day you asked me to be your *sahwira*?' He shook his head. His stick trembled in his raised hand. He seemed spent of energy. The elders did not look up. They sweated and blew their noses as if they were snorting AIDS from their bodies. 'I should have known ...' Muchena licked his lips and observed the various groups of mourners who sat around the fire. His head turned slowly from left to right. In a passage between the durawall where women sat singing a long mournful dirge he saw a group of young men whom he had not noticed before. In an instant, he limped towards them.

Midway he stumbled upon bricks that lay in disarray on his path. He winced in pain but did not fall. Support came in the form of one of the pillars of the veranda. 'It will be years before you see a blooming flower in this yard.' He raised his right leg to ease the pain in his booted foot.

'I don't think you even returned the drum you borrowed for the last funeral.' His voice was low and sad. Like a wounded dog he stared down at the mourners who said nothing. Moving back toward the group of young men, he demanded, 'Where is Chimimba?' The small assorted group of bachelors and newly-weds took a step backwards.

'I am sick of the faces of your dead,' Muchena raised his stick above them. 'They say "Die young and look good in the coffin. But your son's corpses are thin and wasted.' He drew back suddenly as if the corpse of Chimimba's son lay before him. The young men kept their heads down. They were grieving their relative, their friend or perhaps themselves. They appeared unscathed. They looked healthy but the atmosphere about them was rich in vulnerability, death seemed to hover over them.

'Use condoms! Condoms! Condoms for safe sex!' Chimimba broke through the young men's thoughts. 'On radio and television you are reminded time and again. There are stickers and posters everywhere like road signs. Chimimba, your sons' ears are plugged, their eyes are blind.'

The youths did not sit in a circle around the fire like their elders. It seemed every one of them was facing the direction from which he expected danger. In their minds they accused Muchena of being a loud-mouth set to brand them as he did the dead. Some thought, 'Why give this lecture at a funeral? Who are you, after all? To hell with this *sahwira* business.' Yet others seemed to accept that their fate had been pronounced. They leaned against the wall, cupping dropped jaws and staring blankly at the ground.

'Where did you get that one?' a young man asked, pointing at the sheathed walkin- stick. He was attempting a show of courage, an air of normality, but his tone was fearful. Muchena smiled and tried to answer the youth.

'They are issued free, these condoms. All over the country. Hospitals, NGOs, social welfare organisations … even beerhalls.' The young man sank his face into his mug. Beerhalls, beer gardens, the palaces of his many mistresses. Images of women flashed before him. He did not remember if he had ever used a condom when he took them to bed.

'Bulls are known by their scars. Chimimba, your bulls are now carcasses. Find someone else to do this grisly job.' Muchena cast a dismissive glance at the young man. One lit a cigarette from the stub of another that he had just smoked. *Sahwira* Muchena walked over to the porch and peeped into the lounge. The room was full of wailers. Women. The widow, the mother, the mother-in-law, sisters, aunts, cousins of the deceased, even perhaps mistresses, who was to know? They wailed like hired wailers paid to impress. Their songs were full of grief. They were seated on the floor as one congregation engaged in one dutiful act of mourning – real mourning, real mourners.

Muchena stood at the door. He raised his metal walking-stick. The rubbery sheath was still stuck at its tip. He could not find standing space in the room so he shouted over their heads from the door: 'Chimimba, I am sick of sleeping out in the cold, away from my wife … because I am attending funerals … your funerals.' He swung his condom stick above the heads of the women. They did not stop wailing but their heads turned from left to right and their mournful gaze followed the stick's path.

'Use condoms. Condoms for safe sex!' His voice broke through the wailing. The women appeared confused and stopped singing. Then it dawned on the mourners that the sheath was a condom and when Muchena repeated, 'Condoms. Use condoms for safe sex,' the drummer rose swiftly, covered her face with her chitenge and left the room. A youngish woman of twenty giggled. The urge to laugh was so potent that it only required one loose mouth to trigger uncontrollable laughter. The young group of mourners scuttled for the passage that led to the kitchen as the sounds of their amusement erupted. The condom had turned out to be something to laugh about. Or something laughable. Perhaps the condom had removed sadness and brought happiness.

The commotion disturbed the women who had been assigned to cook food for the mourners. Their eyes, filled with curiosity, turned towards the kitchen. Operations ceased mid-air: chopped tomatoes fell into a drum, a knife was held poised above the cabbages, flames died down in the makeshift hearth without a hand to fan them. A short stout woman hurriedly tightened the knot of the towel which secured her baby on her back. Otherwise the cooks stood stock still.

'This *sahwira* is going too far.' The remark rose above the laughter, an indignant elderly female voice continued, 'This is not how it's done!'

'Muchena! Go away. Leave.'

'What are you laughing about? Are you not ashamed?' Elderly women began cautioning their younger kin.

Muchena walked through to the door of the kitchen where he could see both outside and in. The laughter had subsided and the young women did not seem to know whether they should return to the lounge or wait for more *sahwira* tricks.

Muchena began speaking in a low authoritative voice, 'Women of the world weep not for this one who has departed but for yourselves, because not even the living are safe. Weeping will not cure suffering or solve problems brought about by the scourge of this epidemic. AIDS cannot be cured. It means death, certain death … after a long illness. You have seen the wasted sons of Chimimba. I am sick, really

64

sick. I fear for myself. Such boils, such cancerous skin, a soiled body weak and ridden with diarrhoea. This I am obliged to touch, nay to wash. I fear for myself, and only because I am a *sahwira*. That is why I am now refusing to continue. Chimimba, you must find someone else to clean your dead bodies.' One by one the young women in the kitchen sat down. They listened as if they were listening to the last sermon of deliverance.

'Chimimba! Chimimba!' Muchena's voice was sad. 'When I heard of your son's death, I knew what was expected of me. First to come and pay my last respects. Second to comfort you. I knew I was expected to do all the dirty work but at last I need a chance to speak my mind ...' Muchena stopped as he gave way to the elderly women who began to sing. It was an impromptu song but soon everyone joined in:

*The Lord recognises those who obey him*
*The Lord wants those who obey him.*
*Obedience is better than offerings.*
*Obedience is better than offerings.*

Muchena joined in the singing and his baritone voice filled the room as he moved amongst them. He laid his walking-stick down on the floor. From out of the big pockets of his heavy overcoat, he brought packet after packet of condoms. He handed one to each woman as he walked slowly amongst them, whispering, 'For safe sex, use condoms.'

He whispered like a priest administering the Holy Eucharist. The young women accepted the condoms for safer sex. Some put them in their pockets, others into their brassieres, and others into their handbags and purses.

The mourners sang on, 'Obedience is better than offerings,' and the men outside sipped their beer silently as they warmed themselves by the fire.

# Occasional sex

Occasional sex
without protection
with a prostitute
keeps the body
on its toes
to the cemetery.
Occasional sex
with a prostitute
using condoms
keeps the mind anxious.
You never know
about stretched rubber.

# The shoes of a vagabond

The shoes of a vagabond
can dance alone
and on their own
when her skirt refuses
and clings to the buttocks
in a kwasa kwasa dance.

The shoes can dance alone
when the blouse holds
on to the breasts
in a dance
to the tune of waltz.

The shoes can dance alone
when the beret is adamant
and remains seated
on the head.

The shoes of a vagabond
can dance alone
when all her clothes
cannot join in.

# Deceased

A deceased attended
its own funeral.
It liked the coffin
of oak
with golden handles,
welcomed the mourners
in black fashion
and drenched in tears,
admired the flowers
from who is who
in town,
appreciated the grave,
a cool deep hole
in an upmarket grassland,
but thereafter
retired in its grave
regretted
all that was uttered,
and said in its name.

# 7

# The funeral

The funeral cortege arrived just after sunset when the fowls had come home to roost. The cattle were in their pens. Fires were being lit and the village people were preparing for supper. Life was settling down as darkness took hold of this rural community with its pole and *dhaka* huts and a few brick houses with fashionable asbestos roofs. The cortege, which included a hearse, the last of the old vehicle models, and a bus, snaked its way into a fenced and gated homestead containing a big modern house painted cream. In the flickering car lights, the asbestos roof glowed maroon; in the shadows stood a small round kitchen hut.

The hearse stopped at the front of the porch. People, presumably villagers, came forward to welcome the funeral party. There was a big log fire at the centre of the yard. The four men who'd been sitting around it rose to welcome the deceased and the entourage. The welcoming party sang mournful songs. Those alighting from the bus and the cars wept loudly as they met and embraced their relatives. Thus far, it was a typical rural funeral wake: people wailed and consoled each other as the room in which the deceased was to lie in state was prepared. Most men and women knew each other. Greetings were conducted quietly so as not to disturb the mourners who were gripped with emotion.

'Chemhere ... Chemhere start the proceedings,' came a loud whisper from an elderly man smoking tobacco rolled in newsprint. He glared at the deceased's nephew who'd been given the dubious responsibility of managing the ceremony: part go-between, part master of ceremonies.

'*Vazukuru! Vazukuru* of the deceased! You are required here – quick quick.' Chemhere's voice was authoritative as he addressed the young men who had been told to carry the coffin.

'We are here.' A group of young men chorused as they appeared at the porch lit by the headlights of the cars behind the hearse. The noise of mourning subsided. Everybody was attentive. The gathering wanted to follow the proceedings.

'I beg your pardon, fathers and mothers. I think we have to remind each other that before the box is carried into the house, the fathers or mothers of the deceased should say a few words,' croaked a small bespectacled man who relied on his walking-stick to stress his point. A smell of opaque beer wafted from his pursed mouth.

'No – no – no! If I remember well, those who have to say something according to our customs can only do so once the body is in the house.' Chemhere corrected the man who stroked his small self-important moustache. The young man strode towards the hearse.

'In which house is the body being laid – the big house or the small one?' The owner of this voice spoke from the back.

'I would like my mother to be laid in this house – on this her last day on earth.' A mournful voice was heard and people looked in the direction of a fashionable young man wearing a voluminous white shirt and loose low-slung denim trousers. A buyer and seller of electrical equipment, he travelled up and down to South Africa, and knew the value of sharp dressing.

'But custom dictates that she must be laid in her kitchen, Maikoro, and eh – eh – eh ...' The man shrouded in darkness beyond the reach of the car lights, the invisible adviser, paused to continue ... Maikoro was, after all, the deceased's only son. There was silence for a few moments, then the women started to murmur to

70

each other. They seemed desperate to be heard. They wanted to contribute to the proceedings but it appeared as if they were afraid of their menfolk. The men continued to deliberate amongst themselves, not offering the women a chance to be heard.

'The kitchen is too small to accommodate all of you.' Chemhere was conclusive as he turned the handle of the door on the back of the hearse.

'That's no excuse. How big are kitchens in this village? Are we not mourning our dead in these small thatched huts?' The invisible man argued and the mourners seemed to agree with him. Most quietly concurred that kitchens were often not big enough to accommodate many people and yet it was the custom that the dead lay in state in the small round huts. The kitchen hut was where mourners came to pay their last respects. This was how it was done.

'Let us hear what the elders have to say,' Chemhere backtracked, his eyes searching for an elderly man sitting on the porch. 'Tell us what to do, Sekuru Chaitezvi. You have seen it all.'

'Although I feel I have a contribution to make, I believe that I have no right to say anything before the Gurundoros talk. This homestead is theirs and they are the ones to make the decisions. The woman who lies in the box is their wife. Thank you.' Chaitezvi spoke with restraint as if, should the situation demand it, he could give a thorough lesson on the dos and don'ts of custom. Muttering and the exchange of suppressed whispers could be heard among the mourners.

'Gurundoro, my uncle, we ask you to tell us what to do.' Chemhere, who was master of ceremonies, sounded impatient.

'Maikoro, did your mother indicate which house she wanted to lie in when she died? Because we would also want to respect her wishes.' Gurundoro, clean-shaven and wearing a dark suit and a broad-brimmed hat, was clearly a man about town. The eldest of the Gurundoros of his generation (after the death Maikoro's father) he bore the weight of family responsibility with pomp and circumstance.

'No. She said nothing to me. I don't know if she said anything to my sisters. Did she, Mai Leslie?' he asked.

'No. But is mother going to remain in that hearse for the whole night while we argue?' Mai Leslie sounded angry. A woman in her late thirties, she wore the Catholic church uniform: a blue cloak, covering the neck and shoulders, over a conservative white dress. She held a rosary in her right hand, a thumb and finger on a bead.

'Who said she would have to spend the night in that truck?' Gurundoro retorted angrily. 'Be careful what you say in front of us. Don't rush into things you don't understand. I am the brother of your father and I do not wish to be led by you, a woman.' He removed his hat to expose white hair ruthlessly brushed backwards. His lips twitched in the dim light provided by one remaining vehicle. Other drivers had taken the precaution of conserving their batteries.

'I am sorry, Gurundoro, our father, we have erred, forgive us. Please lead us forward with the proceedings.' Maikoro apologised for his sister.

'I am sorry, Gurundoro.' Mai Leslie genuflected and clapped her hands in apology while still clutching her rosary.

'I am here to bury my sister-in-law not to settle scores.'

'Maikoro, I heard you say that you wanted your mother to be laid in there.' Gurundoro pointed with his hat at the door of the big house. 'Your wish is granted.' He staggered a little as he gave way to the *vazukuru* who hastened to bring down the casket. The invisible man invisibly shook his head and walked away followed by the bespectacled man with the beery breath. The religious women drew back and started to sing a religious song accompanied by a drum that pounded slowly and religiously.

Small baskets and vases of flowers were unloaded. A big white casket with big golden handles was heaved out. The young male *vazukuru* of the deceased were the pall-bearers. They carried the casket to the door. Two men entered the house to receive it from within, but the casket was broader than the width of the door.

'The box cannot pass through, Gurundoro.' Chemhere was calm. 'Place the box down, away from the door. It is heavy.' The younger man treated his uncle with circumspection.

'Ah! What's that, eh?' Gurundoro did not expect anyone to answer him. He walked to the door, studied it, and then gazed at the casket and strode into the house. 'What do we do now?' He slapped his leg several times with a folded newspaper. The women stopped singing and began to mutter amongst themselves.

'She does not want to lie in that house.'

'She wants to lie in her kitchen, in the small round house.'

'Somebody told us so,' a woman said under the cover of darkness and this sentence was passed from woman to woman, as if the deceased had imparted valuable information to them before she died. They were fearful.

'Gurundoro, uncle, when we bought this casket we asked the undertaker if, given its size, it would pass through standard door frames and he assured us that it would. He even carried it through their doors, which are, I presume, the same as these ones.'

'My God.' Maikoro put his head in his hands.

Word spread to the men who still sat around the fire and they came hurrying forward as if macho prowess was all that was needed to make the casket pass through the door.

'We can only do one thing — break the door down,' Gurundoro declared without consulting the men who had gathered in the room in which the deceased was going to lie. The room had already been lit with several candles placed on small plates around the walls. Gurundoro removed his hat.

'How about tilting the box to one side?' An excited voice suggested from the darkness outside.

'No, we are not going to tilt my sister-in-law, the wife of my brother! What an idea! As if there were no other way of getting this box through this door.' Gurundoro spoke impatiently.

The invisible man became visible. He was standing in the lone light of the car. His scant beard and large nose could be seen by all. He stood in full view as if he wanted to address the mourners.

'Let the box through the window,' another voice called out excitedly. The mourners chuckled. Beside the door was a large window without burglar bars. It seemed at a glance as though the casket would slide through it easily.

'Murewa, stop your *sahwira* pranks and mourn your own *sahwira*. Whenever did you hear that a deceased was let into her house through a window like a burglar?' Gurundoro was quick off the mark.

'She wants to do it this last time. She was used to it. Don't you know that she was a witch? Let her through the window and she will be very happy.' The woman who spoke was bent and old but contained a mouth still full of small white teeth. She wore a torn *chitenje* beneath her new blue and white Anglican Mothers Union uniform.

Inside the house Gurundoro and a few elders, including Chemhere, discussed the problem in low voices. The *vazukuru*, the pall bearers, stood quietly, ready to follow instructions. The elders called Maikoro, who listened to what was being said from behind a ring of five men. The large room was, presumably, a lounge. Reed mats were spread over the floor. The room was painted white and a Love calendar strewn with red hearts hung on the wall opposite the door.

'I suggested … rather, I reminded them what they should do when a person dies. We cannot mourn her in that good-for-nothing white man's house.' A voice, inarticulate with anger, burst forth. Then its owner turned on his heel and disappeared. His dog followed him at a distance. It seemed to understand his outbursts.

'What has gotten into the minds of our people? Gurundoro should just instruct that the box be laid in the kitchen, her hut,' the unnamed man said, pointing at the round thatched house. He was visibly disappointed with the way Gurundoro was directing matters.

'Gurundoro, which Gurundoro are you talking about? He does not know a thing. He is a town fellow, that one.' Chaitezvi felt an awful desire to laugh, so he coughed instead as he brushed his scant hair with his palm.

'This way, he messes up things,' said someone firmly. Everyone nodded in agreement. All the men knew what was supposed to be done at a traditional Shona funeral, but none of them were prepared to speak out openly. They complained, and showed contempt for the decisions that were made, but always behind their hands and under cover of the darkness, showing no responsibility for the mistakes that would be made about which they could subsequently feel very superior.

'There is no advice you can give these people. Gurundoro is already drunk. We drank together at the bottle store all day today. He came early to arrange things … and what arrangements has he made?'

An odorous smell of alcohol breathed through Mharapara's impressive nose when he talked. His hands twisted and turned as he played with his faded golf cap that he'd removed in honour of the deceased. A small bottle of brandy exhibited itself in his overall pocket.

'But Chemhere knows everything. At his mother's funeral there were no meetings such as those we are now witnessing here.'

'I do not share cigarettes.' Chaitezvi quickly advised a supplicant who asked for a puff every time he brought out his packet of toasted smokes.

'Chemhere cannot say much – he is still a young man. He will have to wait to be told what to do by the senior Gurundoros.'

'At this rate the body will be sleeping outside in the open.' The chuckle developed into a cough as Mharapara mooched away from the group of men on the porch.

'Mharapara should stop smoking because his cough is really bad. One of these days we may find ourselves sleeping outside as we mourn him.' Chaitezvi followed Mharapara over to the log fire. His *sahwira*, who had seen the bottle of alcohol in Mharapara's pocket, followed quickly in anticipation of being offered a swig.

A sudden quarrel erupted between Gurundoro, the elders, and the young Maikoro. People dispersed abruptly not wanting to be allied to any side with who knows what consequences.

'Do what the child wants.' A determined voice was suddenly heard above the others.

'I am doing what is right, not what that kid wants.' Gurundoro shouted, swinging away from the circle. He walked unsteadily towards the door. The women stopped singing and scrambled to the window to see if a really good fight would develop.

'That child, Maikoro, built this house for his mother, so if he wants his mother to lie in here, let it be.' Mwoyondizvo's beard was long and white. His head was clean shaven and shone in the light of several candles. He followed Gurundoro as he spoke to him but did not show any signs of agitation. He talked slowly and wore a cynical smile. He was the brother of the deceased.

'I am the father here. *Vazukuru*, carry this box into the kitchen hut and let's see if it doesn't go through the door.' His voice was compelling. 'This house belongs to the Gurundoros. Maikoro may have built this house for his mother, but it now belongs to the Gurundoro family.' Gurundoro pointed at the casket with his newspaper, conscious that he was the head of the family and required deference. The *vazukuru* rose but did not lift the casket. Instead they squatted beside it and waited for a conclusive instruction from both parties.

'Please, Baba Gurundoro, I beg you to grant me ... this permission.' Maikoro beseeched his uncle with knees bent and the clapping of hands. The small head above his big shirt and his knee-long trousers made him appear like a large praying mantis.

'I have nothing against you, my son, but it is this brother of your mother, Mwoyondizvo, who wants to impose his authority over me. I cannot allow that,' he shouted, standing above the coffin at the door.

'Please. Let's not do it this way. Let us resolve this issue amicably.' Chemhere raised his hands and hurried to the door. He did not want Mwoyondizvo to come near Gurundoro.

'Let's break the door-frame on one side — get a hammer,' Mwoyondizvo suggested casually. His request provoked Gurundoro who stood fuming at the door, acting as if he wanted to carry the casket in alone. Alternately gesticulating, shouting, stamping his feet and bending over the casket, he was determined to assert his authority. Mwoyondizvo stood at a distance in a fur coat, khaki shirt and trousers. 'What is in that kitchen?' he enquired. 'Tell me what is special about that kitchen? These heathens will believe anything.'

'The box is now going into the round house — I am the father here,' said Gurundoro. 'My brother married your sister and I know very well that he paid all the lobola you wanted. So, leave us alone and let us get on with it. *Vazukuru*, carry the box into the kitchen.' Gurundoro led the way and the *vazukuru* lifted the casket with exaggerated vigour and turned towards the women to make their way towards the small kitchen hut.

There were two candles in the hut where three sad women sat talking, oblivious of the quarrel that was taking place outside. Hearing the *vazukuru* approach, they rose and moved their mats to the door.

'You want me to leave you alone but ...' Gurundoro did not hear Mwoyondizvo's threats but they were overheard by Chemhere and Maikoro.

Meantime, the women followed the casket-bearers. They did not sing, as they should have done, because they were interested to hear how the quarrel developed. They did not want to miss a word. It was a long time since anything so exciting had happened and they looked forward to weeks of gossip after the funeral.

Chaitezvi and Mharapara mumbled something in apparent approval as they returned to the porch. As they saw the casket going through the kitchen door someone whistled and someone else shouted, 'Lay it on that reed mat.' Gurundoro beamed triumphantly and slapped his thigh with his newspaper. Mwoyondizvo walked away to his camp, a group of men who had made a small fire behind the big house. The battle lines were drawn.

'The deceased wanted to lie in her kitchen,' Chaitezvi said, following the coffin.

'She would want us to do the proper thing – the right thing.' Mharapara stubbed out his cigarette and blew away the smoke before he entered the kitchen hut.

'Gurundoro has come to his senses at last.' The invisible man was visible again, rubbing his big nose.

'Gurundoro, you should not buy things from Mbare Musika!' Murewa, the *sahwira*, stopped to laugh aloud. 'At Mbare you do not get things that are up to standard. Look at what's happened now. It's not that the deceased does not want to lie in that big white house. It's that door-frame which is the problem. You should not buy rejects at Mbare, things you get through the back door. Cheap goods are always a problem in the long run.' Murewa burst with laughter at her own joke and was joined enthusiastically by mourners as though they needed laughter to overcome their grief. They laughed until Murewa started to play the drums. She led with a song which forced her religious colleagues to remain silent. 'Why are you not singing? Are you hungry? Do not worry, Gurundoro will do something for you – Gurundoro has plenty of food and plenty of money, though he does not have plenty of sense,' the *sahwira* commented jokingly on their silence. She carried the drum into the kitchen hut where the deceased now lay.

Maikoro disappeared into the darkness behind the small round hut which now housed his dead mother. He sat with his back against the wall and cried. He had longed for his mother to lie for the last time in the house that he had built for her over five long years, and over which his uncle now seemed to have assumed control. He had also bought an expensive casket of varnished oak with golden handles to accord his mother a decent funeral, a respectable farewell. He would not have minded if the door-frame had been broken but Gurundoro had taken charge and the elders had not been sensitive to his wishes. He wept alone. The ground he sat on was wet with the urine of the people who'd relieved themselves behind the kitchen hut. The air around him smelled acrid but he just sat and cried.

He heard Chemhere call his name. 'Maikoro! Maikoro! Gurundoro, where is Maikoro?' He remained seated. He knew that they required him now. The funeral could not go ahead without him, but he did not respond. He had been overlooked, cast aside, his wishes barely considered. He sat still in misery.

'I do not know. I'm also looking for him. When you find him send him to me immediately.' Gurundoro's voice seemed bent on wanting to antagonise the young man further. Maikoro sat with his head between his knees and his hands clasped around his legs. He hated his uncles for flexing their muscles over his mother's dead body. He hated them for settling whatever scores they had against each other at his mother's funeral. He hated them for coming to dictate and for contributing nothing towards the expenses of the funeral. He knew that they engaged in arguments but when it came to paying the penalties they incurred in the process, they expected him to bail them out.

He was aware that his maternal uncle had been rebuffed by the brother of his late father and before everyone. Gurundoro had abused Mwoyondizvo verbally and that was a grievous offence as far as their relationship was concerned. The Mwoyondizvos would certainly not sanction the burial of their sister, and the Gurundoros could not do this on their own. Mwoyondizvo had threatened this when Gurundoro snubbed him. Maikoro knew such a threat was not an idle one. His uncle would certainly cause havoc the next day. And all the Mwoyondizvos would be on his side. They would demand a goat or an ox depending on how the Gurundoros presented themselves before their in-laws. Their desperation would provide the barometer.

Maikoro did not want to return to the mourners, who seemed to be having a good time. There was a good fire, plenty to drink and a quarrel to entertain them. Exhausted by days of preparation and genuine sorrow for his mother's death, he slept.

He was found much later by Chemhere who came to relieve himself behind the round house.

'What's wrong, Sekuru? Everybody is looking for you,' Chemhere said, surprised to find Maikoro in a foetal position, and asleep. Half drunk himself, he staggered and smelt of fresh beer.

'Really? Why?'

'You are a Gurundoro, so you must always be available. If we encounter problems we may require your decision on certain issues – there are issues, Sekuru ... developments, Sekuru ...' Chemhere mused drunkenly.

'What developments?' Maikoro asked still half asleep. He looked up at Chemhere without appearing to show any interest.

'Sekuru, you are sitting on urine – rise – I will get you a beer – come to my car.' Chemhere tried to raise Maikoro and failed. Maikoro was inert, a dead weight, but he propped himself up against the wall of the house.

'What developments – what issues?' he asked again because he expected Chemhere, who was the master of ceremonies, as well as the eldest *muzukuru*, to know if there were further misunderstandings between his maternal and paternal uncles.

'Come along, Sekuru. We will discuss them in my car – my beer is cold.' Maikoro followed Chemhere because he had respect for him. Even though he was drunk, he did not behave like his uncles.

'I do not want to participate in this mess that is my mother's funeral.' They sat in Chemhere's car and drank beer until dawn. They discussed family issues that had been raised at the funeral. Chemhere consoled Maikoro who complained about the bickering and drunkenness of his uncle.

'Gurundoro – wanted me?' Maikoro remembered, stretching himself in the restricted area of Chemhere's small Datsun sedan.

'He said so ...' Chemhere hesitated to divulge what Gurundoro wanted from Maikoro.

'Why?' Maikoro demanded, as if he did not want to have anything to do with his uncle.

'He does not want you to pay for the goat.' Chemhere sounded distressed.

'What goat?' Maikoro laughed cynically.

'Payment for abusing Mwoyondizvo. That family were threatening to leave last night.'

'Who abused the Mwoyondizvos?' Maikoro asked, though he already knew the culprit was his uncle, whose drunkenness violated the culture of respect between in-laws. 'Gurundoro, I suppose.' He pronounced the name as if it was an incurable disease.

'Sekuru, those people mean what they say. They may refuse to mark the grave for the diggers. And no one else can do that. If you don't pay the money, your mother's burial will be delayed, and whose fault will that be?' Chemhere's argument was compelling. He used his hands for dramatic emphasis as he talked.

'Where is Uncle Gurundoro?' Maikoro was about to get out of the car but Chemhere restrained him and handed him a fresh beer from his cooler box. Maikoro was getting agitated. Chemhere did not know what he intended to say to Gurundoro, who was equally excited, but he could see a quarrel developing when two men who had had a lot to drink and hadn't slept, began to insult each other.

'Hold on, Sekuru — you must approach Gurundoro tactfully. One thing for sure is that he does not have the seven hundred thousand dollars required to buy the goat.' Chemhere spoke very slowly. It was hard to tell whether having had too much to drink, he was deliberately trying to appear sober, or whether he thought that speaking slowly would lend weight to his advice.

'I have the money.' Maikoro seemed to have made up his mind.

Later, after sunrise, Chemhere presented the money for the goat and a fowl to the Mwoyondizvo people who accepted the retributive gifts and proceeded to mark the position of their daughter's grave according to custom. Everything proceeded well until after lunch when it was time to leave for the burial. Relatives from both families assembled in the house where the deceased lay for the final rites.

'My daughter, we're now taking you to your final resting place, to your home next to your husband. I hope you will appreciate all that has been done by your people, especially your children, who bought the box, the blanket, the goats for *chema*, the cow for *chirariro* and the cloth for *fuko*. Go well, my daughter, we will meet in the life beyond. Do not forget your children. Look after them. Death is not the end but the beginning of a sacred life.' The oldest member of the Mwoyondizvos clapped his hands lightly to end his speech. Mourners clapped their hands and nodded their heads in approval of his words. The reverent atmosphere in the room encouraged communication with the deceased. Several people then spoke to their late sister, cousin, aunt ... until Chemhere called a stop to their recitations. The casket was opened and the relatives circled round the body silently saying their last farewells.

Outside the house in which the deceased lay the women sang and danced. Some sat in the shades of the fruit trees: a big aged mango, a peach and an avocado pear. They talked casually to each other but maintained an air of solemnity. The men settled in groups farther away. They complained about the slow pace at which the Gurundoros were conducting the funeral, even though they knew that a proper burial ceremony needed half a day.

'It is already twenty past one,' Mharapara announced as he looked rather obviously at his plastic watch, which was the only one in the whole village.

'We do not want to rush the burial. There are huge stones to be laid. We want to follow the correct procedures at the right pace.' Chaitezvi picked his teeth. They had all eaten a good lunch with big chunks of meat and sadza. 'It's time to go to the graveyard,' he said with a knowing expression.

Then Chemhere appeared at the door of the round kitchen hut. He clapped his hands to attract everyone's attention. Everyone stopped talking. He clasped his hands to his chest as he addressed them.

'The headman, councillors, ladies and gentlemen. The time has come now for the deceased to be taken to her final resting place. But before we leave we shall place the box out here in the yard so that you may all view the body one last time. After that we will proceed to the graveyard. All the speeches will be given at the grave. Thank you.' Chemhere disappeared back into the house.

The casket was carried into the open by the *vazukuru*, dressed in black suits, and led by Chemhere carrying a reed mat. The mourners fell into single file and waited to see where the casket was to be placed. Then, as the pall-bearers strode slowly towards the porch of the big house, the base plank of the casket fell to the ground, followed by a big bundle wrapped in a blanket and white cloth. The pall-bearers, boys in their late teens, panicked and dropped the casket on top of the deceased, and then fell away in fright, aghast and disclaiming. Chemhere strode forward with reverent steps like an undertaker leading a funeral procession, oblivious to the accident that had befallen the deceased.

The singing women and the mourners proceeding behind the casket screamed and scrambled to hide behind each other. Chemhere turned his head. His mouth fell open in disbelief as he saw the casket lying on top of the deceased.

There was a moment of complete silence. The men stared at each other in shock. Everyone was afraid and poised ready to flee should it become necessary. Gurundoro, who had not formed part of the procession, appeared from behind the round house, walking resolutely, his newspaper and hat in one hand, towards the frightening heap. He observed the casket and shook his head slowly. The lid was closed. Below the casket he could see his dead sister-in-law's toes. Single-handedly, he tried to pull the casket away from the body. Maikoro, in a trance, stood staring at his uncle, his hands in his pockets.

'Don't just stand there, doing nothing,' Gurundoro grumbled without looking at his nephew, but his voice was firm and it seemed to reach Maikoro who moved towards the casket. Uncle and son then each took the casket's handles and lifted the large white broken box off the body.

Murewa, the *sahwira*, of the Mukanya totem, strode purposefully towards Gurundoro, who seemed unsure what to do next. She burst into her usual laughter, but her face streamed with tears.

'Gurundoro! Gurundoro! You always want to give us the impression that you are rich. But what's this?' she shouted, securing her zambia around her waist. 'You call this a coffin? I told you not to buy cheap things made to look grand to appease us. Who are you trying to fool?' She cried again aloud, and then began to ululate and dance in front of Gurundoro who had bent over the body. 'Look at your box. A Zhin' Zhan' box Gurundoro! Zhin' Zhan' box Gurundoro, Zhin' Zhan'' she repeated in song. The tension eased and people started to laugh, in suppressed bursts at first but in no time they were laughing aloud, and clapping their hands in unison.

'Zhin' Zhan' box Gurundoro! Zhin' Zhan'! Zhin' Zhan' box Gurundoro! Zhin' Zhan'!' The *sahwira* continued to sing, pointing a mocking finger at him.

'Let me spread the mat in the house.' Chemhere bore the reed mat into the big house as if he was carrying a log on his shoulder. The mourners who sat in the shade of the porch rose and rushed out of his way as if he was a ghost. Gurundoro did not argue when he saw Chemhere entering the house. He just watched and waited.

'We cannot leave *ambuya* in the sun. We must carry her into the big house.' He said to himself as he came back out of the house. 'Let's lift up *ambuya*, Uncle Gurundoro.'

The body was wrapped in a white cloth and a blanket, and picking up the corners of the blanket, they began to lift the body. Mharapara moved to help them. Maikoro's mother was carried gently into the big house followed by Murewa the *sahwira* who was still chanting, 'Zhin' Zhan' box Gurundoro! Zhin' Zhan'! Zhin' Zhan' box Gurundoro! Zhin' Zhan'.' Mai Leslie, Maikoro's sister, walked slowly behind Murewa. The religious women began to quietly follow them in, and the rest of the mourners, gathering their wits, moved slowly into the house.

It had not been the funeral they'd been expecting, and they would talk about it for years to come.

# I do not want to be mother

Mother seldom claps
to cheer
but often claps
to rebuke.
Her hands
are always full
of slaps and claps.
She sends me
to bed with a hug,
but hauls me out
next morning –
as if I refuse
to attend kindergarten,
my refuge.
I would not spend
a day beside her
if it were possible.
She pats me off
at the school gate,
but demands to know
how I fare,
and expects grand results.
She buys toys, many toys,
but keeps them locked up
when I need them.

*Because she is the one*
*who buys them*
*the toys remain hers.*
*When I am hurt*
*'I hurt myself'.*
*When I cry*
*I am 'making noise'.*
*She is a mother.*
*She is quite big.*
*When I grow big*
*I do not want*

to be a mother

# Commission of Inquiry

The Commission of Inquiry
appointed to probe,
the Commission of Inquiry
set to investigate,
the Commission of Inquiry
that recommended the establishment
of a Commission of Inquiry
to examine the findings
of the Commission of Inquiry
whose Commissioner died
before presenting a report
was last night disbanded
to make way
for a downsized
Commission of Inquiry
led by the Chief Justice
to make an inquiry
into the same.

# 8

# An early supper

**The minister concluded his speech** bellowing slogans, party slogans.

'Down with AIDS!' The honourable Minister of Health punched his fist towards the ground.

'Down!' A five-hundred-strong multitude shouted their response, their fists similarly punching the air. They were relieved that the long speech had at last come to a much desired conclusion.

'Down with child abuse!'

'Down with it!' The thunderous response was of a people happy that at last they could go home and because they knew they were all under the watchful eye of the party youth on the look-out for anyone who remained silent. Punishment was meted out immediately without much regard for the law enforcement agents who also mingled with the crowd. The youths were armed with sticks, iron bars, sjamboks and bicycle chains.

'Down with sugar mummies!' The comrade minister stamped the platform with his twiglike legs.

'Down with them! 'Tthe strong party colours — green, yellow, red and black — dominated the regalia, as most people were in their shabby and nondescript best.

'Down with sugar daddies!' The comrade minister was not yet through. He wanted to emphasise all society's atrocities while he was at it.

'Down with them!' The crowd howled in response. At times the crowd livened up the spirit at these meetings by being mischievous, but not today.

Comrade Chipikiri, the Minister of Health, had come to Norton to present the HIV-AIDS funds to Tahwina District. The money and the truck were supposed to be presented to the town of Norton, but had found their way into the coffers of a party district: a whopping two hundred and fifty million dollars for prevention programmes, home-based care, medicines and materials. In his speech, the Minister emphasised the need for abstinence. An overhaul of social behaviour was called for — not to mention total respect for the African culture.

The District Chairman closed the meeting by advising the multitude to be vigilant in identifying cases of child abuse and reporting them immediately.

'Down with child abuse!' The chairman repeated the minister's slogan.

'Down with it!'

'I am sorry, Comrades. I forgot to inform you that you will be told in due course how this money will be disbursed. The branch committees will be called in for the final assessment in two days' time. You are free to leave.' That was enough to send the people jumping and scuttling away to freedom. The crowd disappeared with miraculous speed, except for the party youths who were always on the look out for enemies of the party or the state. They kept a watchful eye on such meetings. These were held on an empty patch of ground surrounded by houses. Being central, it was a convenient place in which to herd people who had long lost interest in attending meetings. A crowd could be force-marched to the venue without causing the youth too many problems.

'Comrade Seguranza and Comrade Chipoko, organise your guys. All the roads must be sealed. It is time for private meetings,' the District Chairman ordered.

'Can I have the drinks for the youths, Comrade Chairman?' It was party tradition that after a meeting, the  faithful should be treated to drinks. Seguranza Mabhunu had looked forward to spending the rest of the day drinking beer.

'The welfare department will sort that for you. Make it fast — we do not want to delay the Comrade Minister.' Seguranza Mabhunu, who was accompanied by three youths, collected crates of opaque beer and soft drinks and distributed them to the other youths situated at strategic positions around the venue.

The minister relieved the plank platform of his weight. He was a heavy mass with a fleshy trunk and very short limbs. His waist would have needed a medical practitioner to identify it. He looked like a potato bearing four short stumps. He walked casually, his legs slightly apart, over to a group of district cadres who were waiting to greet him.

'We thank you for remembering us. Ministers rarely visit us. You are the only one who really cares,' the cadres chorused, showering him with praises as they shook hands with the great man.

'You are welcome, sons of the soil,' he acknowledged as he stood in front of them. He stood on his toes and stretched himself like a pig that had learnt to stand on its hind legs without support.

'Comrade Mondo, you look great in that beautiful scarf.' He embraced a thirty-eight-year old woman, crushing her intimately against him. The woman wore a white T-shirt with the head of state emblazoned on the front. The hem of her white skirt was high above the knees like that of a tennis player. The scarf around her neck sported the bright party colours. Mondo shrank into his embrace.

'Thank you, Chef.' She gave him a blooming smile that prompted the minister to rub and then pat her shoulders. He released her while continuing to hold her hand with both of his. Then he stared piercingly into her face as if he were seeking some assurance about an issue they both understood. Comrade Mondo could not handle his stare. She looked down.

Mondo was a widow, but many people knew her as a divorcee. She did not want people to conclude that she was a carrier of the deadly disease, which they might if they knew that her husband died. She had a captivating smile, was very light in complexion and had a trim body that flourished in all the right places. At thirty-eight she had gotten used to widowhood and become accustomed to the perks of being single. She would even on some occasions borrow her daughters' skirts and wear them with girlish abandon. She was the district women's league chairperson. Long plaited locks strayed onto her face.

'That was a great speech.' She knew how to control a situation, which could easily get out of hand, by drawing the minister back to the purpose of his visit.

'Please, I would like to have a — a — word with you before I go — lest I forget — please remind me.' The minister released her hand and passed on to the district treasurer.

'OK,' she replied knowingly. The curious knew that she had some secret dealings with the chefs but they did not know what such deals involved. Cadres who'd been interested in the conversation, pretended to look elsewhere.

'She is now after the minister,' women cadres whispered to each other.

'That way she can feed her children and send them to school.' The onlookers sounded envious. They muttered and whispered.

Mondo had three school-going children, two girls and a boy. All of them commuted to Harare every day where they attended expensive private schools. As she was not known to have embezzled party funds, it was clear these fees were paid from a different source.

'Her former husband is paying maintenance through the children's court,' a gossip enthusiast said, clapping her mouth with her palm to avoid being overheard.

'Which husband? Her husband died of AIDS.'

'You are at it again, Comrade.'

'I am telling you the truth, she is a carrier,' the first woman whispered into her comrade's ear. The gossip raged on. Their curiosity was always in top gear. Speculation was scintillating.

'Comrade Treasurer, we would like the books of accounts for this project to be very well maintained to avoid misuse of funds,' Comrade Chipikiri advised a very short man holding a big black hard-covered tome enscribed 'Cash Book' as if he was carrying a suitcase. He listened with the air of a Grade One child who still found his teacher fascinating.

'I will ... you will not complain.'

'I am thinking of bringing in my nephew who did a Chartered Institute of Accounts course — an advanced course, to help you with the books because this project involves a lot of money.'

'Ah ... ah ... yes — to help me of course.'

'He will only come in once a week to balance the books. You will do everything

'... the day-to-day transactions will be handled by you.'

'That makes it easy for me.' The treasurer did not elaborate.

'You will pay him, of course – just a small fee, transport, lunch, etcetera. He will write monthly reports on the finances for head office. A financial report can only be done by a qualified financial expert.' Comrade Minister pressed on completely oblivious to any offence he might be giving.

The drinks were served. All brands of clear beer were available. Soft drinks were in short supply in most beverage outlets but that was not a problem because all the cadres drank alcohol. Most wanted the hard stuff like brandy which they drank without water.

Comrade Chipikiri was presented with his favourite whisky which he personally prepared with soda water taken from his Mercedes Benz. Cold meats, biltong and potato crisps were washed down the throats of the comrades by the abundant alcohol. And soon the volume of the comrades' voices rose.

'Do we have anyone with a driver's licence who is not employed?' Chipikiri asked the district chairman who had joined the group. Almost everyone was holding a brown bottle. Chipikiri clasped his glass delicately as if to stress that the contents were sacrosanct.

'Is there someone with a driver's licence? Class four?' the chairman shouted at the top of his voice. No one responded.

'We must have someone to drive the truck,' the minister explained as the room quietened a little. 'If there is no one amongst us with a licence, I will bring my cousin, an ex-combatant. You will pay him.' Comrade Chipikiri wanted to show that he was on top of the AIDS project.

'I know of someone who has driver's licence. He is not working,' a female committee member said, gripping the neck of her bottle like a cooking stick.

'Is he a party member? Who is he? Do I know him?' The chairman was full of excited questions.

'He attends meetings ...' The woman was at pains to explain the credibility of her choice, and then took a swig to avoid further questions.

'My cousin is a war veteran,' Comrade Minister declared firmly, to dispel any further suggestions.

'He is the only one suitable. We are not employing sell-outs; no opposition party members,' the chairman blurted his opinion, before guzzling the last drops from his bottle. He put the empty into a crate and opened another bottle with his teeth, so much more efficient than an opener, he thought. 'Do you still – e – e – e?'

'I will have some more – e'. Chipikiri emptied his glass. A generous amount of whisky was poured into it and topped with a little soda water. It was a secret shared by many that the minister travelled with a goodly supply of alcohol in his Benz.

Comrade Mondo showed up, next to the chairman. She had a fresh beer. The other cadres moved closer to her and cocked their heads. They hoped to glean more about the relationship between the two of them.

The minister's attention suddenly switched. Mondo's sporting outfit seemed to mesmerise him. Surrounding comrades, ears pricked, pretended to be deeply engaged in their conversations.

'I understand the girl who recited that AIDS poem is your daughter,' Comrade Chipikiri said, as he surveyed Cadre Mondo from the head down to the shapely legs in cream sneakers.

'Yes, Chef. My second-born.'

'What form is she in?' He stood facing her, consuming all the charm she exuded without having to crane his neck.

'Two.' She was a woman of very few words, but she thrust her ample chest forward as she spoke.

'I'm glad that you asked your child to grace this occasion, a community cause – Comrades!' He raised his excited voice to draw the attention of an already attentive group. 'Comrades, it only shows how committed some of our cadres are to party issues. Comrade Mondo excused her daughter from school so that she could participate in launching this project. I will definitely see that she gets a reward. She must be rewarded. I am a man of my words.'

'Thank you, Chef.' Mondo rewarded the minister with an intoxicating smile.

'This is amazing. Call the TV crew, no, the chief reporter.' The district political commissar, bottle in hand, trotted to where the crew was packing their equipment into a mobile TV van.

'Did you record that girl's poem on camera?'

'Yes, sir – eight o'clock prime news slot.' The reporter knew what it all meant. The minister was known to have an unquenchable passion for publicity, especially through the electronic media.

From a distance groups of youths could be heard singing war songs. They were strategically positioned at entry points to the meeting venue. The volume and the lyrics to their songs showed that the youth were competing to impress the minister. The opaque beer was greasing their broken voices and enhancing their natural talent for song composition. Indeed they executed their duties with a zeal that compromised the safety of even party members.

The minister was slightly drunk when he finally summoned his chauffeur for the drive back to Harare. Before he left, the chairman shouted, 'Bottoms up!' He finished the little beer that was left in his bottle. The minister also cleared his glass. The political commissar held the half bottle of whisky, the glass and an unopened bottle of soda water. The group of officials led by the chairman and Comrade Mondo accompanied the minister to his car.

'Send the girl to my office tomorrow afternoon,' Chipikiri shouted as the black Mercedes Benz drove slowly out of the protected area. The secret between the minister and Mondo was out. The district officials knew the girl was being invited to the minister's office.

'I will. Thank you, Chef.' replied Mondo.

The man of the people was tipsy. He exchanged effusive farewells. The group started to sing. They were happy. The women's league chairperson was their leader. They admired her efforts. The group bade farewell in song and then got back to the business of drinking as soon as the car was out of sight. It was quite a party.

Mondo was a slow drinker, but she drank until late that evening. She left, drunk, but still managed to carry half a crate of her favourite beer, two kilogrammes of braai pork and four packets of potato chips.

***

Dorcas, Mondo's daughter, walked into the minister's office accompanied by his secretary. The latter knew that the girl was expected. Chipikiri had informed her, though he had forgotten what time he had suggested.

'Thank you. OK. OK,' the minister mumbled when the secretary ushered Dorcas into the room. She knew that she was no longer required. She knew her boss. She saw many young female visitors enter his office. She was past curiosity. She guessed what happened beyond the closed door.

'Welcome. Welcome. Feel free, young lady. What is your name?' Chipikiri stretched out his hand to greet her.

'Dorcas. Good afternoon, Sir!' She stood upright, her legs together like a school-girl who had been summoned to the headmaster's office, but did not know why. She wore a white short-sleeved cotton blouse, a pleated Crimplene blue skirt and a boater. From her shoulder hung a big blue satchel full of books. She was as smart as she could be in polished black shoes and white socks.

'I was very impressed with the poem you read. Sit down.' The minister did not sit down. He put both hands in his pockets and see-sawed on his toes and heels. 'Did you write the poem?'

'Yes, Sir!'

'You must be very bright.' Dorcas did not know how to respond, although she had rehearsed how she was going to react, smile, stand and laugh. Her mother had gone through the paces with her before she left for school that morning.

'I will not consume your study time for long.' The man pulled open a drawer and sat down. He produced two fat wads of brown bearer cheques accompanied by a wide smile. 'Here, have this. Two million dollars, but I think your mother must know about this show of appreciation. You must participate at these meetings and I will certainly reward you for your efforts.'

'Thank you, Sir. I will tell mother.' She beamed. Her eyes concentrated excitedly on the two bricks of bank notes. She stretched her youthful lips and broke into a grateful smile.

'You are welcome, young lady. You will earn many things. I believe in rewarding people for services rendered. One day you will be happy you met me. You can leave, but come next week, Wednesday. Same time. I will arrange something good for you.' He talked fast, swallowing his words.

'Thank you very much, Sir.' She clapped her hands in appreciation. Comrade Chipikiri took out a big manilla envelope and placed the money inside. Then he moved round to the front of his desk and stood beside Dorcas for a while.

'I want you to be careful with this money. It will be safe in the satchel with your books.' The girl took the envelope tremulously. She unzipped her bag and after a little struggle, shoved the envelope between the books. She was trembling. Chipikiri could see that her fingers were not steady. 'Best regards to your mother. Do not forget to tell her that she must visit me when she is free.' He stretched forward and kissed Dorcas on the forehead. It was just a peck. She did not squirm. The early morning rehearsal with her mother had included such a kiss, and her mother had told her to sit quite still, even if his breath was hot or smelt of whisky.

Dorcas was about to rise when the minister said, 'No – don't – e – e –' My secretary will take you out.' He went back to his desk and phoned his secretary in the next room. Sitting down again, he smiled at the girl as if he was smiling at his mistress, an indulgent, self-satisfied smile. The girl looked away. The secretary rescued her from his scrutiny, and the minister busied himself with a few papers on his desk.

Comrade Mondo was not at home when her daughter returned. She was a full-time party worker; a full-time volunteer. She was involved in all the women's projects – poultry projects without chickens; piggery projects without pigs. Projects, projects, projects. They brought women together to learn party propaganda. They became adept at singing party songs and chanting party slogans. Since the presentation of the AIDS funds Comrade Mondo wrote a new register of the party faithful. She collected all the information she required. She visited all the AIDS patients and orphans and compiled a list of who was a member of the party. All the ward, branch and district executive members were eligible for the fund as office bearers and workers. The officials would not get the same amount. She knew from experience that no one was going to scrutinise her efforts. She made certain that everybody in the party got something and that members of the opposition realised what a sacrifice they were making, for even if they had one or two or more AIDS victims in their homes; what mattered was a party card, and party attendance, not ill-health.

'Mother, the minister was wonderful.' Dorcas greeted her mother with the news when she arrived home. Her mother, undoing her colourful party scarf, beamed with delight.

'Really?' The older woman regarded her daughter incredulously. How could the minister be wonderful to her teenage daughter? 'OK, save your breath. I must change first.' She disappeared into her bedroom.

'How can the minister give you that much money?' Lydia, her older sister, asked

Dorcas. 'Why? For a poem?' The girls discussed the visit as they paged through a few old fashion magazines, wishing they had thin elegant figures like the models in the pictures.

'I guess he just has lots of money.'

'You should be very careful. This could lead you somewhere you …' She stopped when their mother re-entered the lounge having changed into more comfortable old clothes.

'Now tell me, how did you … You did not shame us?' She sat on the sofa next to Lydia, and facing her youngest daughter.

'The minister wants you to visit him again soon.' Dorcas' voice rang with happiness.

'I will certainly do so. Did he keep his promise?'

'Mother, what promise? He gave us two million dollars!' Lydia's tone was as amazed as it was doubtful. She wanted her mother to say something that would explain it. She could not understand the minister's generosity, and it made her anxious.

'Two million what?'

The older woman drew away from Lydia and clapped her hands in disbelief.

'Mother, Comrade Chipikiri gave me two million dollars.' Dorcas pulled the manilla envelope out of her school bag and handed it to her mother. Lydia watched her mother's reaction closely.

Mondo looked at the envelope, then she opened it slowly and saw two big bundles of bearer cheques. She did not take them out, and put the envelope down slowly.

'Minister Chipikiri is a man of his word.'

'What word?' said Lydia.

Her mother did not answer. She seemed to have recovered from her surprise. 'Did you behave?' she asked. 'You did all things I told you to do?'

Lydia opened her mouth to say something. How could her mother accept such a gift as genuine? How could her mother trust Chipikiri's generosity? How could she ask if Dorcas had presented herself well? Would he have given the money to her sister, if she'd been rude?

'Did you thank him?' Comrade Mondo asked Dorcas.

'Of course, Mother. I clapped my hands and genuflected.'

'But I still can't believe it. How can one earn such an amount of money, just from reading a poem, and not even a very good poem,' Lydia persisted.

'It is possible. It depends.' Mondo did not elaborate. Her voice was emphatic, as if she would brook no further discussion.

'Such money is dangerous ....' Lydia rose and went out to prepare supper. 'It's just how sugar daddies attract young girls,' she shouted from the kitchen.

'He promised to do something for Dorcas ... Eh — everybody knows about this. They overheard him. So I do not see anything sinister about the gift.'

'Can I have something to drink?' Comrade Mondo continued as she approached the fridge. 'How soon is supper?'

'An hour,' Lydia replied, as she chopped the onions more vigorously than usual.

'You will cut your fingers,' Mondo warned her daughter. Lydia threw the onion into the pot as if she was discarding rubbish in a trash bin.

Mondo poured some Mazoe into a glass, added water and drank a little to taste the mixture. She sat down on a chair and slowly began to drink her juice. 'You can share the money, you two. Don't tell your brother, though. And put three-quarters into your savings account. It is a long time since you saved anything.' Her voice was loud enough to be heard by Dorcas who was still reading the fashion magazine in the lounge.

'Dorcas, put that envelope in my wardrobe.' Lydia knew that such instructions were final. 'Don't you want a drink?' Mondo offered a general invitation, her attention on Lydia who had sat down and put her head in her hands. Mondo pretended not to notice her discomfort,'Go on have an orange juice,' she said.

'We've had some. Don't you want a beer? There are still twelve beers in the fridge,' Dorcas said when she joined her sister and mother in the kitchen.

'No. Where is your brother?' Her question was directed at Lydia but the older girl looked away.

'He has gone to the shops. His fish has run out of flakes.' Simba, the youngest of the Mondo siblings, had a sizeable fish tank in his bedroom.

Comrade Mondo lived a comfortable life by high-density standards. She never ran out of food. Her children were never sent back home for failing to pay school fees. She owned expensive furniture, domestic appliances of good quality and she ran a late model Mazda 323. She was not driving the car because the country was experiencing fuel shortages. Her dead husband had left nothing of note. His few material possessions worth anything had been collected by his relatives. They had abandoned his widow and the children after she had refused to be inherited. So Comrade Mondo had been left with an empty house in Highfield and three small children. She sold the marital house and bought one both cheaper and larger, forty kilometres west of Harare in Norton. She made Norton her home.

The following Wednesday Dorcas paid Comrade Chipikiri a visit, as per his invitation. 'Just be careful,' Lydia warned her sister when they parted after lunch-break. Lydia felt strongly that she ought to go with her, but she was captain of the tennis team, and couldn't excuse herself from the afternoon game. Dorcas assured her that she was big enough to protect herself.

'How are you, young lady? You look gorgeous in those sporting shorts.' The minister squeezed her shoulder after his secretary had retreated to her office.

'Thank you,' she murmured as she took a seat. She wore a tight white T-shirt, white shorts and white takkies. Although she was coming from the hockey interhouse tournament, her hair was neatly tucked behind her head, with hairpins. She carried a satchel and a hockey stick. 'Mother was grateful for the gift – er – money.' She smiled. Her face showed that some recent touches of face powder had been hurriedly applied. Her mother had again lectured on self-presentation.

'I have some more money for you …?' It was a statement that sounded like a question. Dorcas opened her mouth but immediately covered it with her hand in evident surprise. 'Five million dollars.' He stood beside her, see-sawing on his toes. 'Give me your bag – and I will put it in your satchel.' He took the bag from her, went around the desk, opened a drawer and placed five bundles of brown bank notes inside the satchel. He studied her reaction as he displayed each bundle before he put it into her bag. Her first thought was that as Lydia had suggested there was something going on between her mother and the minister. Some affair. She concluded that she was being used as the conveyor of gifts between the two. They were too magnanimous to be hers. He brought the satchel round to her. A waft of alcohol crossed her nostrils when he came closer to her.

'There is a school in America where bright girls like you can enrol and go up to university level. I will e – e – e – what do you intend to do – law, medicine, commerce, science, education?' His voice was authoritative. He waited for her reply and enjoyed watching her breasts move tautly below her T-shirt.

'Education — teaching.' She moved her chair backwards, away from the minister, away from the alcohol.

'Professor at university — Professor Tracey Mondo! How do you like that? If you wanted to pursue medicine I could assist you — that is my line, you know. You could teach medicine eh eh um. ' He had forgotten her name.

'I need assistance but not yet.' She was blunt. She was discouraging the performance in which Chipikiri was engaged.

'Why? There is no time like the present. I can send you to the States, to the Big Apple, to go to high school — I have ... all my children are overseas.' He rubbed his palms against each other and swung his short legs sideways.

'I will think about it.' She rose. the minister was drawing too close to her. 'I will ask mother.'

'That's what a bright girl does.' He rose from the desk and whispered into her face, 'I am available if you need my assistance. You can go to America — any time.' It was a loud whisper.

Then his left hand stretched to cup her breast. His right hand encircled her waist and drew her to him. His breathing intensified hoarsely and suddenly he seemed to have run out of words.

Things could have gone the way he wanted had the girl not panicked. She vigorously dislodged herself from his grip and pushed him away from her. He staggered back drunkenly because he had had too much whisky during lunch at the City Citizens Private Club. The girl moved away from him, picked up her bag and hockey stick. The minister lunged towards her but he missed and fell to the floor.

All this had happened quietly, even his laugh, as he chortled, 'You like a game do you?' and grabbed her ankle with his hot pudgy hand.

Unthinking, she seized her hockey stick, and struck the minister three times on the back of the head with the bent edge of the stick. Then almost weeping, and still feeling his sticky fingers round her ankles, she hurried out of the office, closing the door quietly behind her. She thanked the secretary, who was not surprised to see tears, she had seen them so often before, and proceeded to the security checkpoint without raising any suspicion or alarm. In no time she was out in the street, where she ran all the way to the bus terminus for Norton commuters. Her one wish was to get back to her mother and sister and the safety of home. As if she expected someone to follow after her, shouting, she kept looking back over her shoulder.

She met her mother at the gate of their home. She was holding her satchel like a shield and her hockey stick like a rifle. She felt like a soldier who has run away from battle.

'Whatever is the matter, Dorcas?' Her daughter's face was dark and taut.

'That minister of yours.' For the first time since the attempted rape she began to cry. Comrade Mondo took her satchel and hockey stick and they walked into the house together. Mondo put her arm round her daughter's shoulders. 'Tell me what really happened.'

'He is a brute, a drunk.' Dorcas shook her body as if she was shaking off the minister.

'Tell me in the house.' Comrade Mondo found the keys under the door mat and opened the door. Dorcas was trembling. Her equanimity gave way to fear and shock. She was, after all, only fifteen. Mondo gave her a drink, saying, 'You'll be all right, Dor. You'll be all right.' Her mind was working fast. How far did he go? She had almost expected him to go the whole way. Her mind had not let her think beyond this.

Now, there were consequences, and not the ones she had anticipated, however unconsciously.

'First of all, Dorcas, we will hide this money in the chicken run.'

Mondo took the money out of the satchel, deposited it in a big plastic bag. Then quickly she moved outdoors and shoved the bag between the corrugated iron sheets which were the roof of the fowl run.

'From now onwards,' she told her daughter firmly, 'the minister did not give you anything. When they come you must admit that you hit him but only because he was about to rape you.' Mondo was calm, pragmatic, calculating. She would prefer the police right away, to the covert retribution later. They would have to move, and would anywhere be safe?

'Are they going to arrest me?'

'No. Routine questioning. I'll come with you.'

'But I hit him three times with my hockey stick.' Tears rolled down her cheeks.

'I will be with you, Dorcas.' Mondo held her daughter in an embrace until Lydia came.

'I knew it,' said Lydia angry and despairing, as soon as she saw her sister and mother together on the sofa. 'I knew it.'

'He didn't hurt her, Lydia. He didn't rape her.' Mondo defended herself against the unspoken accusation.

'Prepare an early supper. I don't want the police to arrive before we've eaten.'

# Shrapnel

During mass uprisings,
food riots, work strikes,
bullets missed him
but shrapnel wounded
his mind, his spirit.
He talks
in his sleep
of ambushed mouths
full of assaulted words
that cannot define
their agony,
words slurred.

# Recipe

*Take a sizeable number*
*of township residents*
*adults of varying ages*
*cram them into a combi*
*until full*
*allow time to heat*
*from high-density suburb*
*to industrial hub*
*transfer into factory*
*steam for eight hours*
*stuff back into a combi*
*leave none behind*
*when settled down*
*in matchbox houses*
*let mixture simmer*
*and then allow to cool*
*in bed at night.*

*May be served as bad temper.*

# Victoria Falls

The Victoria Falls
is where the magnificence
of the Creator is manifested.
Nature celebrates its wonder
in a huge waterfall
without the luxury of myths
the Mosi oa Tunya
is how the splendour
of the Lord is exalted
the rainbow rises
from earth to heaven
forever and ever
the glory of his majesty
thunders in the cataract.
Hosanna to the Highest
Glory to the work of His Word
Alleluya! for once
God showed off.

# 9

# The Commuter

It was an October morning. The sun at 6.30 a.m. already felt hot. I walked fast, taking short quick steps to the bus stop. I leapt across a stream of raw sewage without covering my nose or holding my breath. I was used to spewing sewage. Every morning and every evening I leapt across this streaming leakage which came from a manhole in an unfortunate resident's yard. It flowed across the path and along the school durawall to a storm-water drain, three houses away. I was so inured to its presence that I just leapt like a frog over human waste. Faeces. Broken or intact. Raw and rolling. Swept by water. I saw this every morning on my way to work. A morning without sewage was not my morning. Mental breakfast.

I arrived at the bus stop when three combis were loading up. I took advantage of the jostling and scrambling at the terminus. It was a huge scrambling fight as people tried to board the mini-buses. There was the semblance of a queue but very few people recognised its purpose. It seemed everybody wanted to leave at once in the same combi. It seemed everybody was late for work, forty miles away in

Harare. I found myself inside a red vehicle. How I managed I'm not sure. But my feet didn't touch the ground until I was inside. It was a daily routine. Work actually began at the bus stop. I had become adept even if I lost shirt buttons in the process.

There was nothing one could point to that indicated that the area was a terminus: the central Norton terminus. It was simply an open space of ground cut through by a tarred road that ran from Chinhoyi to Harare. A chain of vending stalls constructed of wooden poles and sacks made the terminus appear more like a market place. The vendors sold anything that was in short supply: sugar, soap, cooking oil, diesel, petrol and mealie-meal. Items rarely found in the few shops situated behind the stalls. These goods carried black market price-tags, and these changed every day. Engine oil was also sold in plastic containers which once sold beverages, and fish vendors supplied fresh fish from the nearby Darwendale Dam which they kept in rows of buckets.

There were no signposts to direct commuters one way or another, no shelters in case it rained, and no parking area. The combis loaded and offloaded their passengers randomly within the open space. There was a service station nearby adorned with big red fluorescent lights, but it had passed its use as a re-fuelling station for diesel, petrol and oil. It never received its supply of these commodities and was slowly becoming derelict with grass growing around the pumps.

The bus-stop was constantly full of people waiting for transport. In fact, the place always seemed like a rally with a great multitude of jostling people waiting impatiently to be addressed by a very important person.

The authorities always made certain that they collected money for use of the terminus from the mini-bus drivers. A council official armed with a baton stick and a receipt book approached every bus that arrived. There was no telling what services the operators were paying for.

I sat at the rear seat of the combi which I shared with three enormous women who had bulldozed their way into the bus without regard for human flesh or adornment. They had shoved or pulled aside anyone who was in their way. If they tore shirts and jackets in the process well that was just too bad. They puffed and chuckled triumphantly. I was squashed like a child in the corner between hard metal and soft burgeoning flesh. I kept my face to the window.

Norton had become a dormitory to Harare's workforce. Although the journey was expensive, we could do nothing about it because most companies had shut down in our little town that had once held so much promise. In addition, Harare had a housing shortage.

The excitement that follows achievement had died down. The victorious occupants slowly fell silent and a few individuals immediately fell asleep.

'My bosses, it is now time to pay up,' the conductor growled. We were travelling fast along the Bulawayo-Harare highway. The conductor held onto the sliding door of the omnibus with his right hand to maintain his balance. His big reddened eyes regarded everyone accusingly as if we were all potential cheats. I heaved myself out of my tight, wedged position to fish my wallet from the back pocket of my trousers with my two fingers.

'*Vabereki*, make sure you pay the exact fare because I have no change. This is our first trip this morning. I don't want to delay you by running around looking for change when we arrive in Harare.' He addressed us as relatives and bosses but his words were a far cry from his attitude, which was that of a prison warder. I was lucky because my wallet was still there and it still contained one intact blue bearer cheque. Many people lost their valuables during the jostling process. It was always advisable to hold one's wallet with one hand whilst using the other to beat one's way into the bus. But my cheque was for five thousand dollars and it was all I had. The fare to Harare was two thousand five hundred dollars so I needed change if I was to make the return journey.

The big woman took my bearer cheque from me and gave me change for the return journey. It was assumed in the general camaraderie of bus protocol that she would use the balance to pay my fare. I sighed with relief. But when I wanted to resume my seat, the little space I had acquired had gone. The woman beside me had gained ground.

'You can fit in, *Mukuwasha*.' I looked at her, confused. I did not know what she meant by asking me to 'fit in'. For the first time I observed that she was wearing a see-through blouse and her pumpkin-size breasts were threatening to burst out of her bra. A yellow crocheted mini skirt exposed a half petticoat and rather large thighs.

'Move aside just a little,' I begged her, nudging her plump leg with the side of my knee.

'Sit, *Mukuwasha*, sit,' she ordered patting her thigh. I obeyed. I sat down like a rider, her breast soft against my back. And that very act defied my apostolic church beliefs, which meant that I would be required to make a full confession in front of the whole congregation at church service the next Sunday. My reflexes were not helping me. I did not rise immediately.

'*Mukuwasha*, can you really ...?' I rose with speed aware of the trouble I was getting myself into. I turned my head to give her a reproachful look. Her eyes, heavy with eye-shadow, a large open nose, rouged cheeks and red lipsticked lips were moulded into a smile that vindicated me. I looked beyond her to her two equally enormous friends.

'Let him sit down, Rachel,' the woman in a pink jumper dress and a fanciful hair-do chuckled. Rachel moved just a little.

'Sit, *Mukuwasha*. You will fit in.' She insisted. I squeezed myself slowly down between Rachel and metal. Remembering that I was an apostolic, I once again turned to stare out of the window. The combi was cruising fast. I sat like a boy fascinated with the passing scenery, although I saw it twice every day.

'Back seat, did all of you pay?' The loud growl woke me from my stupor. I cast an inquisitive look at the big woman beside me. She took my money and I did not notice how much she passed on to the conductor. 'Brother, did you?' Different sets of eyes turned on to me and I was suspect.

'Yes, I paid for him.' Rachel said loudly. I felt like a kindergarten boy on a bus trip with his mother. I was glad she'd been so quick to rescue me, although I knew she erred when she said that she had paid for me. At that moment I noticed a bold yellow sticker above the window of the bus: 'Those who do not pay lose their teeth.' I felt my teeth with my tongue. They were intact. Combi conductors were known to be ruthless, aggressive. They would not hesitate to do grievous bodily harm to an errant passenger.

'I paid and you gave me change.' I shouted in panic. Rachel gave me a reproachful look. I turned my face to the window.

'*Hwindi*, count your money well before you start fingering passengers – are you new to this business?' She rose and pointed a threatening finger at the conductor. She was reacting as if she was my next of kin. She did not want anyone else to make any exchanges with the conductor. 'I gave you two blue bearer cheques for the rear seat.'

'I am sorry — I know where I missed …' He did not sound sorry. He counted his money again and wrapped it into his green trouser pocket. His white T-shirt was grey with dirt and emblazoned with a picture of a man with bulging muscles, the wrestling type. Rachel leaned back squashing me again. I felt cramp in my leg.

To wile away the time I began to read the stickers: one above the driver read, 'How is your wife and my children?' Another, 'If you are drunk, no problem but do not be a problem,' which confused me. What did it mean? 'Beer is better than a woman. You can have it in public.' I found myself giving the conductor a long critical look. How could he be so obscene? How could he defy all forms of decency? How could he be so provocative? But naturally I could not say anything; I did not want to lose my teeth or limbs.

We had reached the roundabout near Kuwadzana high-density suburb and with the increasing traffic, we began to slow down. At the flyover on either side of the road new houses were being built. Beautiful houses. But the maxim about my wife and his children gnawed at my mind. Were my children not mine? Were they someone else's children?

I had two beautiful daughters who loved me. Girls who shared my life. Cheerful girls. My daughters. I loved them. Of course they were my offspring. I trusted my wife, Juliet. What was the sticker trying to achieve? I did not appreciate the humour.

I felt a jab in my ribs. '*Mukuwasha*, we've arrived.' The fat woman elbowed me. 'I know they're all mine.' The words slipped out of my mouth. Rachel gave me a brief suspicious glance. I looked away. I followed her out of the combi. She moved slowly, sideways like a crab.

When at last I alighted, I could not walk. My cramped leg would take no weight. I sat down on the kerb and stretched my leg forward and back. The pain slowly eased. I rose and half running, half limping hastened to work. I was fifteen minutes late.

# Run black girl

Run black girl run,
torn breasts drip blood.
Run, black girl,
there is nowhere to hide.
The bushes have been burnt,
fathers hid in the mountains,
mothers hid behind clay pots,
you have nowhere to go.

Your jingling bracelets are noisy
wriggling hips upon the wind.
Run, my girl, run.
You are losing us,
cosmetics like sand
can be washed away.
Hear.
Lovely fingers wear no rings.

Doves are known by their coo,
virgins by their laughter.
Run, my girl, come.

# In the beginning

In the beginning
was the Word
not many words.
As a result
creation was not chaotic.
The Word
had not yet lost meaning
for man was still an embryo.
His tongue
had not yet developed
its fork.
In the beginning
God should not have
rested
until discipline
was instilled.

# From a painting

*After a sleepless night*
*a woman's mind*
*asks a toothless baby*
*cradled in her arms,*
*are you my fault?*

# 10

# The Employment Agent

*'Neeesi! Neeesi! Neeesi!'* The call was dull and sickly. But it was too desperate to be ignored in the dark hospital ward. The lights had just been turned off and the patients were silently preparing to endure their ailments through the night.

'Who is calling?' An alert nurse rushed from her well-lit office into the ill-lit ward containing twenty male patients. A light from the office filtered into the wide passage between the two rows of beds.

*'Neeesi! Neesi! Neeesi!'* It was a protracted call and full of pain.

'Tendai, what's troubling you again?' The nurse switched on the lights and a few patients groaned as they were jolted out of the soft darkness. The nurse ignored their complaints.

*'Neeesi* the chamber!' Tendai appealed. He had plaster casts on both legs from his toes to his thighs. Another cast covered his bent arm from the fingers to the elbow. Punctured lips, four missing front teeth, and a bandage that covered his right eye and forehead showed that his head had not been spared.

'Okay Tendai.' The nurse drew on her plastic gloves. She pulled the curtains around Tendai's bed and helped him to urinate.

'I am sorry, Nesi Nkomo.' Tendai always apologised during the ablution process. He was ashamed to be attended by a woman but he could do nothing about it.

'It's not a problem, don't hesitate to call me,' Nurse Nkomo reassured Tendai as she drew back the curtain. She disposed of the contents of the chamber pot in the toilet. 'Good night, Tendai.' Her cheerful voice was accompanied by a wide smile. She was always open with the patients, which is why they knew her name.

'Thank you, Nurse. Good night.' She switched off the lights on her way back to her office. Darkness descended on the accident ward.

'Mrs Nkomo is a nice lady — not like that sharp-tongued whore who drives me mad,' said the patient in the bed next to Tendai's. He groaned noisily as he turned on his side to face his neighbour. 'What actually happened to you?' he whispered loudly. He wanted to talk, to pass the time away. Sleep did not come easily. 'A car accident?'

'I was assaulted by a mob.'

'A mob? Why? Where?' his voice was hoarse, but he spoke with the speed of a reporter who feared to lose his interviewee. It was the first time they had talked in three weeks, beyond exchanging greetings.

'I'll tell you tomorrow — I have a terrible headache ...' Tendai didn't want to talk: a headache always attacked him at night, just after the lights were switched off.

'The day you arrived, you looked terrible.' Suddenly, despite his aching head, Tendai wanted to look at himself in the mirror. For the first time in three weeks he wanted to know what he looked like. He could only imagine a toothless face and a swollen eye. He felt pathetic.

'The doctor says I may be discharged soon,' the man said happily as he lay on his side facing Tendai. Tendai could only stare at the ceiling. He could do nothing else. Occasionally, and with difficulty, he would turn his head towards his neighbour.

'How long have you been in here?' Tendai asked, wishing that he could also leave soon, though he knew that even then he had nowhere to go.

'This is my third month — complications with my broken jaw have held me back, otherwise I should have been long gone. You should have seen what I looked like when I came in. The doctors were very professional. They said, 'Mr Dube, we are not letting you go until you can talk. And, as you can hear, I am now speaking.'

* * *

The doctor had finished his morning round; his examinations and remarks were encouraging. He had said that Tendai's eye was healing fast. The young man complained that something — he thought it was lice — was biting him in the casts — a horrible sensation as he could not scratch his limbs. The doctor said it was more likely a heat rash and promised to bring him some soothing powders.

Now that his jaw was better, Mr Dube was animated and tried again to pursue his conversation with Tendai. 'Tell me, what happened to you?' he prompted. 'You said that you were going to tell me this morning.'

'I posted three election campaign posters on walls at a business centre,' Tendai began his story. 'I was in Mabvuku. I was about to stick a fourth on a wall opposite a vegetable market when I saw a mob approaching, but I did not think they were coming for me. They walked quietly but fast, one or two were women with babies on their backs. I carried on applying glue to the wall. I did not imagine that they could be coming for me. I just wanted to complete my job. Then, suddenly, I was attacked from all sides. The first blow was to the back of my head and I hit the wall with my face. I don't remember resisting or fighting back. It was like a whirlwind. I must have passed out at the first blow. The next thing I knew I was in this bed.

'Posters? For which party?' Mr Dube was interested and he sat up a little.

'I don't remember the party but I remember the name of the person who contracted me to do the job, a Mr Masenda. We share the same surname,' Tendai explained, oblivious of his naivete as he tried to dig his finger into the cast for a good scratch but failed to reach the irritation.

'But how did you come to know such people?' Mr Dube asked. The lunch trolley rattled as it was wheeled into the ward and the smell of cooked cabbage, meat and sadza wafted all round the big room. 'Lunch time already?' Mr Dube exclaimed, squeezing his nose several times with his thumb and forefinger as if the smell was revolting.

'Lunch is most welcome — I'm starving.' Tendai rubbed his belly and swallowed. He enjoyed his meals, having been fed on fluids for ten days. He looked forward to sadza now that he could eat again.

'The smell of boiled cabbage upsets my stomach,' Mr Dube declared. He rarely ate hospital food because his family brought him everything he needed. Tendai could not complain that he found the food revolting because otherwise he would starve. His relatives still had no idea that he was in hospital.

'My folks don't know that I'm here,' Tendai said pursuing his train of thought.

'But how were you engaged on this campaign?'

'I was not campaigning — I did not campaign. I do not belong to any party. I was only hired to put up the posters. I didn't have a job and I needed the money, that's all.' Tendai explained slowly.

'Where did you meet, this Masenda guy?' Mr Dube pressed on. He sounded as though he did not quite believe Tendai.

'I'd spent seven days sleeping in the street with nothing to eat. You know the sanitary lane behind Pam's Hotel in Third Street — the bins there are always full of left-overs so we always converged there with other street people — I could not help it. I had to learn the tricks or starve.' Mr Dube lay quietly on his bed. Tendai's voice faded as his mind revisited the streets of Harare. 'It was in the morning around 8 a.m. when the bins were still full of breakfast left-overs. I was picking bread, fried eggs, sausages and chips from a trash bin when a man with a big bald head smiled at me through the window of his car. I had not heard the car approach because it barely made a sound. Quickly I picked up my bag and my folded plastic sheet and piece of cardboard and ran down the service lane because I thought he might be a sugar daddy or a plain clothes policeman.' The municipal police harass the street people every day. The man reversed his car slowly down the lane keeping pace with me. I was very frightened and about to drop all my things and bolt when he called, 'Tsano! Tsano, you want a job?' His voice was friendly and insistent. I stopped but kept my distance. I did not trust him. 'Job?' I asked and my voice gave me away because it sounded hopeful. I've been looking for a job since I left school three years ago. The man switched off the engine of his car and smiled again.

Bald head said that he had a job for me. It was as if we had known each other for a long time but I had never seen him before. He did not get out of his car but he told me that he was looking for someone to employ and meant me no harm.

I told him that I was new in town and I did not have anywhere to stay. He assured me that the job was mine and he would definitely find a place for me to stay. He told me to wait for him whilst he went to buy some food. He seemed kind. I was suspi-

116

cious, but I needed work and I was hungry.

Before he went to buy food, he introduced himself as a Mr Masenda. He chuckled when he found out that our surnames were the same. I couldn't believe it. I told him that I came from Rusape. I was quite excited. I thought we might be related. But he told me that that discussion was for another time.

'He must have watched you for a long time,' Mr Dube suggested. It seemed unlikely. Why would a business man waste his time watching a street kid?

'Really, at that moment, I did not care. All I wanted was a job and money to pay for my fare home to Rusape. I presumed that Masenda was well off. He had a beautiful metallic grey car. A double-cab with mag wheels and High Rider written on the front.' I thanked my ancestors for rescuing me from the streets of Harare. I even assumed that Masenda could be an uncle or a cousin.

He soon came back with food. He invited me into his car, and he did not want me to leave my luggage behind. Then he gave me a Coca Cola, and a box of chicken and chips. I ate the food sitting on the back seat. The radio was playing and now I remember there was something about an election.

'He told me what he wanted me to do, gave me the a roll of posters and some glue and dropped me at a side road that led to the Mabvuku Shopping Centre. He said he thought it would take me a couple of hours to get the posters up, and told me to wait for him at the Mabvuku turn-off when I'd finished. He said that he had to rush to an important meeting but would be back to collect me. He drove away with my luggage which he said would be safe in the car.'

'Now, after all that has happened, do you think he was telling you the truth!' Mr Dube was as sceptical as he thought Tendai had been naive. He did not think that anyone, not even someone who was hungry and homeless, would be as stupid as the wounded young man beside him.

'Why?'

'Don't you even understand now? I would have thought you'd realise why you were assaulted,' Mr Dube said with a mixture of pity and irritation.

The food trolley was pushed right next to Tendai's bed. Mr Dube pulled his sheet over his nose. Really the smell of boiled cabbage and sadza was too much. The orderly arranged Tendai's pillows and helped him prop his back into a sitting position. He lowered the small pulley and his legs rested more comfortably near the bed.

'What are we having for supper?' Tendai asked the orderly, evidently enjoying the steaming food. He sliced a morsel of sadza with his hand, dipped it into the stew and threw it into his mouth.

'Young man, why do you always want to know things that you're not supposed to know? You will know what you're given at supper time. Eat, now. Enjoy your lunch.' The orderly was a small, thick-headed guy who enjoyed his leisure. He regarded the patients as problems that made his work more difficult. He preferred the corpses that he wheeled to the mortuary: they, at least, were not talkative.

'What's wrong with asking what we're going to have tonight?' Mr Dube baited the taciturn attendant.

'And what will it change — if I tell you?' The orderly groaned like a patient and wheeled away the food trolley swearing quietly.

'That man is only fit to work only on a psychiatric ward,' Mr Dube whispered to Tendai, who chuckled.

During visiting hour in the early afternoon, Tendai lay observing the people who sat and stood around each bedside. Flowers, cards and drinks were bounteously offered to sick relatives. Tendai never had visitors. His family in Rusape had no idea what had happened to him and now that he was well enough to ask someone to phone on his behalf, he'd decided that the shock really would be too much for his mother.

Mr Dube's relatives enjoyed the rituals and the attention that hospital visits bestowed on them. The girls saw the ward as a fashion ramp, swaying and strutting down its long length, while the older women competed in offering nutritious recipes and titbits to each other and to Mr Dube. The adult males stood detached and amused behind the women and watched their showy performances. They concentrated on their cell-phones so as not to miss that all-important call, and played computer games.

As Mr Dube now considered that he knew Tendai and felt pity for him, the older man shared his visitors' gifts with him. Dube's relatives always brought too much food. As the young man ate, Mr Dube bragged that his relatives regarded him as their spiritual leader. 'At the beginning of each year,' he said pompously, 'I hold what you may call an annual general meeting with all the members of the family, at which meeting I advise them on important issues such as death, disease …'

So over the next few days and weeks, Mr Dube and Tendai got to know each better and enjoy each other's company, even though the former was thirty and the latter only twenty. Fate had thrown them together and they accepted each other in this interregnum in their lives, knowing that when they left hospital, they would be unlikely to see each other again.

One day, Mr Dube, prompted by something he'd seen in the newspaper, said, 'Could you identify Masenda if you met him again?'

'Yes. He still has my bag,' Tendai reflected in an aggrieved tone. He was not actually sure that he would recognise Masenda, but he did not say so. It would depend on whether he was in his car or not.

'You must claim damages for the injuries you sustained while you were in the process of executing his job,' Mr Dube volunteered. His suggestion showed he was a man of the world. He was, however, doubtful that such a claim would succeed, as there had been no contract and Masenda would simply deny knowing the young man. On the other hand, he considered that if Masenda was a politician, his name or his face would one day appear in the newspaper, and he, Dube, was interested to know more about him.

'I come from Rogoyi village in the Rusape communal lands,' Tendai told Dube. 'I'd only been in Harare a few weeks. He was, Dube concluded, a typical rural youth whose education, like his resources, was very limited.

'Do you have any relatives in Harare?' Dube asked him one day.

'No. I don't know — honestly.' The young man now seemed to realise that there was a great deal he did not know; his stay in hospital had broadened the confines of his world.

'But why did you come to Harare without making any prior arrangements?' It seemed too much for the older man to understand.

'My headache's back again, Mr Dube. I will tell you tomorrow. It's a long story.'

* * *

The next morning, as they enjoyed a cup of tea, Tendai said, 'I came to Harare with the intention of finding a job. A cousin called me to town. He said there was a job in his company. But he had been transferred to Bulawayo before I arrived. He did not notify me.' Tendai tucked himself into the blankets. 'The weather was getting colder as winter drew on. I had no money to go back to Rusape, and nowhere to stay.

'I'd sold a bag of groundnuts to raise money for the fare.' His voice broke. 'My father did not want to give me his blessing but my mother insisted he do so. I remember him saying "I have dreaded those streets…" Now I know what he meant. I slept on the pavement wrapped in plastic and cardboard.'

He stopped wondering how he would ever get home. He thought of Taurai, his kid brother, Tambu his baby sister, old Masenda his father and Matora his mother. His mind wandered down the small path that snaked from his family compound to the well, past the fields to the stream where he took his daily baths. The small family farm of fifteen acres was productive. He had been assured of a decent life in his father's homestead.

'It must have been quite an experience, living in the street.' Mr Dube broke into Tendai's thoughts

'The first three days were really tough. I was hungry and cold, and the other street kids were suspicious of me.'

'Tendai, what would you do if you met Masenda?'

'I really do not know. He has my clothes.' Tendai had not really thought much about what he would do when he left hospital. He had no money, nowhere to go, and he would not be strong. Perhaps he ought to ask Mr Dube to contact his parents. He could write them a letter. Tendai sighed. Every time he thought about the future, which was rarely, he felt overwhelmed.

'You could claim compensation for your injuries …'

'Money for the job I did — but I did not finish it,' Tendai responded. 'What I would like would be my ID, which was lost when I was beaten up, and my O-level certificate which was in my bag.'

'Tendai? You are so …' Mr Dube could not find the appropriate word. He picked up his newspaper.

Tendai lay and thought of home. Harare was not a place that he wanted to be. The huge concrete buildings stared inhumanly down on the people below. Cars were big, loud and fast. People were impatient and rude. He wanted to go home.

Mr Dube rustled his paper. Then suddenly he sat up, 'Maiwe!' he exclaimed. 'Look, look at this.' His finger poked at the paper. 'Here take it,' he threw the newspaper over to the other bed. Tendai heaved himself upright; picked up the paper and patiently marshalled the disassembled pages. Dube was impatient. 'Turn to page three,' he said. 'PAGE THREE!'

Tendai turned the pages, his eyes glancing slowly over the pages as he turned them, and stopped immediately at a rather dark passport-size photograph of Masenda in the middle of the page.

Beneath it was a short story. 'The candidate for Upper Harare constituency, Mr Masenda, was killed by a mob of rowdy youths who trapped him in his car and set it ablaze. His body was burnt beyond recognition. The police apprehended four youths in connection with the case. Violence has claimed the lives of 289 people and more than 5000 people have been injured since the election campaign began.

'The police are appealing to the people for a violence free campaign. A detailed report will be published when police have released vital information concerning the tragedy. It has however been ascertained that the rivalry among the candidates is formenting this violence.'

Tendai closed his eyes. Now he had lost all hope of getting his clothes back. Election, election. He wondered what election they were talking about.

# She

She wore
a thin small blouse
                    that
exposed the edges
of her explosive breasts.
A naked navel
kept me at the edge
                    raring.

Above a skintight
pair of see-through pants,
a water mark stranger
showed
small fleshy buttocks
parted thighs
open like night.

Restraint noticed my excitement.
It sneaked away.
I heard myself utter
to a stranger
words I would never say
even to myself.

Do you like?
I would like.
Would you like
a night out?

# Glossary

*aiwa* – no

*amai* – mother

*chema* – money contributed towards a funeral

*chirariro* – evening meal

*chitenje* – a wrap-around-

*dhaka* – soil, wet soil

*fuko* – shroud

*hondo yeminda* – war for the land

*hwindi* – tout

*kongonya* – a dance common during the liberation war

*hozi* – grain store

*maiwe! /maiwee!* – an exclamation of surprise or horror

*makorokoto* – congratulations

*mukoma* – brother

*mukuwasha* – son-in-law

*mupfuti* – indigenous tree;

*musasa* – indigenous tree; brachystegia spiciformis

*muzukuru* – brother-in-law, term used to indicate friendship/
        kinship

*neesi* – nurse

*pamberi* – forward

*pasi* – down, down with …

*pasi nevatengesi* – down with sell-outs, traitors

*pfutseke* – go away, an expletive.

*sahwira* – a very respected family friend, particularly of the father
        or head of the household.

*sekuru* – grandfather; honorific for an older man

*tete* – aunt

*tske* – a quick curse

*vabereki* – parents, relatives; term of respectful familiarity

*va* – honorific, Mr.

*vazukuru* – grandchildren; respectful term for younger people